A

JOURNEY

DEWITT C. TREMAINE

Copyright © 2025 byDeWitt C. Tremaine

ISBN: 978-1-966954-52-1 (paperback)
ISBN: 978-1-966954-53-8 (hardcover)
ISBN: 978-1-966954-54-5 (epub)

Library of Congress Control Number: 2025910784

Book Titles by

DeWitt C. Tremaine

Ethar World Series:

1. The Rise of a King – Book One of the Ethar World Series

2. A Time for Change - Book Two of the Ethar World Series

3. A Touch of Earth - Book Three of the Ethar World Series

4. Savage Continent - Book Four of the Ethar World Series

5. A Journey - Book Five of the Ethar World Series

6. Tallund - Book Six of the Ethar World Series

7. Telsa - Book Seven of the Ethar World Series

8. When Nothing Happens - Book Eight of the Ethar World Series

9. From Kendlar and Back Again – Book Nine in the Ethar World Series

Touch of Earth Saga:

1. Touch of Earth Saga 1 Heroes

2. Touch of Earth Saga 2 Secret Camp

3. Touch of Earth Saga 3 Janet

4. Touch of Earth Saga 4 Candy

A Journey

"It is time to make plans, Lyamy." Melina the messenger for ShadowDancer an Ancient of Ethar stated.

"Plans? Am I dreaming in the middle of a blink?" Lyamy looked around. She was standing by a statue of ShadowDancer, ancient or goddess to the outcast and those who do not belong elsewhere. The statue was made of metal and gems and was absolutely stunning. Behind the statue there was a cave, concealed by vines. "Why has the goddess sent her lovely messenger?"

"I am not actually here." Melina blushed, "I slipped into your dream, yes in the middle of your blink of rest. This way I can talk to you without actually coming to your home."

"Alright then, what plans are you talking about?" ShadowDancer had given Lyamy the ability to get a full night's sleep in just a blink of her eyes.

"Your journey and eventual arrival in her homelands." Melina seemed to think that explained everything.

"ShadowDancer only made a vague reference made a while back that someday I would see her homelands. I was not previously aware that this was a journey I would be taking." Lyamy was not confused, but simply did not know before now she would be going on a journey.

"Forgive me, then, I am just a messenger. I have gotten ahead of myself thinking you already knew more. It will not be a direct journey there are others you must help on the way." Melina seemed to be trying to figure out where to start over from.

"Is this going to take a long time and am I going to have to leave my den." Lyamy was a Shadowkyn and they were a cat humanoid race, and the den was their family unit. A den could have multiple adult males and females along with cubs and children that completed the family unit.

"Do not worry, you will be able to be in both places at once the way ShadowDancer taught you. You will want a cloak with a cowl that will conceal your identity as needed. Let ShadowDancer know when you are ready. She would like you ready before two weeks have passed."

Lyamy bowed her head slightly to Melina acknowledging her authority to speak for ShadowDancer, "I am the avatar of ShadowDancer, always ready at a moment's notice to do her bidding. You can let her know."

"You will receive further instructions when you reach Kelleeshia." Melina faded and Lyamy opened her eyes sitting on the edge of her bed. The rest of her den was still asleep. She quietly stood up and slipped into the other room.

Lyamy put on clothing that was appropriate for unknown adventuring. She had anticipated possibilities and had a backpack as ready for other climates as she could prepare. She equipped all her weaponry: her clan sword, the two special swords she had crafted, two daggers, a belt with twelve throwing knives, her blow tube, blow darts, composite bow, throwing stars, and arrows. She pulled out the cloak Nelk had made for her from the horvalka hide. The horvalka was a beast that had a magical quality in its fur. Nelk managed to harness the magic when crafting the cloak with the help of a tailor the clasps controlled the effects of the magic. It had a cowl and would serve well.

Shadowkyn did not normally wear anything on their feet. Their feet were more cat like then human; they walked and ran on their toes. She had a special pair of boots tailored for her as gift by a friend. They were elven crafted and offered minimal obstruction while still offering some protection for walking the streets. She put them on, they would help conceal her when she was in the foreign lands.

They used some, but not a lot of coin exchange in Jenyin's Sanctuary, her home. She had several pouches of coins she concealed in various places in her garments. She understood she would need them where she was going. Her friend Marrianne had picked out a few magic items from the storeroom for her to take also. She had been wearing the rings for weeks now, just to get used to the differences they made. The one on her right hand gave her added strength, not that she really needed it, but she had to get used to controlling it. Fortunately, she had not broken anything important. The ring she wore on her left hand was supposed to improve her dexterity. She already had extremely good dexterity and agility and did not notice a change, but on the chance, it might help she kept wearing it.

The items were all made from arcane crafting. The third item was an amulet that increased the toughness of her protective gear and warded off things that might otherwise cause her harm. She did not know if she would need it, but it would not hurt to keep wearing it. It was also pretty, although she wore it under her garments so nobody else would normally notice.

She was ready. She performed the ritual in her mind and stepped out of herself. She turned and looked at herself. It did not matter how many times she did this, it always felt strange being in two bodies and two places at the same time. The farther apart she got from herself the easier it was to keep the two identities separate, so she headed out the door. The her in the den took everything back off and went back to bed with the rest of the den. The other headed to the portal room. The guards let her pass without question. She looked around the portal room. In the center of the room was the original portal they had built opening access to the rest of the world through the city of Kelleeshia. Since the original portal several others had been added one for each of the Shadowkyn centers on the savage continent so that they also could have access to the other side of the waters.

She stepped up to the portal. She had only been through this portal once before and that was when it was built. She had reinforced the arcane magic that opened the portal with the primordial power of the old magic. Lyamy used the magic of the Ancients to see the threads of power at work, suppressing the flames that normal displayed in the eyes when using such powerful magic. She altered time then stepped into the portal, so she could see what she passed as she traveled through the portal. She saw much more than she had expected. There were the threads of power and the flow of folds in time and space which she knew were there. She was moving and perceiving faster than the portal and was able to view things in the dimensional overlaps as she passed though. It would take her time to absorb what she saw, both living and non-living.

She received a gracious greeting as she stepped from the teleport and back into the normal time stream. "The Magus is expecting you. This way please." A man in fancy colorful clothing bowed formally and waved her to follow. She noted aside from the pointless colorful clothing the man seemed to think rather highly of himself based on his airy mannerism. She just nodded and followed.

*   *   *   *

*

Mathew was twelve. He hid in a flour barrel when his mom told him to hide. He watched and heard through the cracks in the barrel as the rogues came and took his mom. "Yer ole' man will pay well for your return when he gits back from the savage lands with a share of the kings treasure." One of them had said as they dragged her away.

He had been living on his own for a month since. Last night he finally tracked down one of the brutes that he saw that night. He was confident he recognized the man as he walked out of the Crowsblood Tavern and followed him to the alley about five blocks away. His dad, Micheal, would be returning soon to Ehrbron with the military detachment. He had volunteered with the military because they needed the money and there were not any other jobs that paid enough to cover rent and feed the family. Mathew wanted to at the very least be able to tell his dad where they were holding his mom when he returned.

Mathew was still small and could fit in tight spaces. The alley was dark, and he was afraid, but it was his mom he was looking for. Both his parents had told him the Ancients of Ethar never answered humans because they are not from this world. This was one situation though anything might help, so he looked up and asked for anyone to protect his family and bring them back together. He moved from shadow to shadow, concealed from view in the tighter spaces between crates, barrels or whatever cover he could find. He positioned himself where he could see the three doors in the back end of the alley and waited, watching and listening.

Eventually his patience paid off. Out of the door on the opposite side of the alley came another of the men who abducted his mom. When the man vanished around the corner leaving the alley Mathew crossed the alley, jumped up on a barrel and looked in the window. The room he looked in was empty and looked like a kitchen. He could see the hall from the kitchen door inside. He ran to the other window on the other side of the door. From what he could tell the only windows would be the two that opened to the alley and three of the five men were in the second room with a window. He was careful not to look longer than he needed to get the lay out. He was standing on the cover of the wood or coal chute when he looked in the second window.

He heard steps coming to the door and quickly dodged into hiding again. Two of the men stepped out talking as they walked.

"We have to take good care of her, we do not want an angry soldier after revenge."

"Yeah, we just want the ransom. He is new to the military and will probably not risk a fight."

"Yeah, unless we hurt her, then he may recruit some of the more experienced soldiers to help him get revenge."

"Don't be so paranoid. Normally we would slit her throat, and then his after he paid the ransom. Who knows, maybe the crow will still call for their executions."

Their voices faded as the disappeared around the corner. Mathew headed back home, he needed to draw everything he knew and come up with a plan. If there was any chance, they might kill his mom, he had to do anything he could to stop that. He sat on the floor finishing every detail of what he knew or could surmise from what he saw. They used fuel in a dug-out chute, they probably dumped the ashes in the under-city sewers which would be another way in and out. There were possibly two small rooms at the other end of the hall or one big room. The sewers were a maze of low tunnels under the city that were cleaned by the rise and fall of the ocean tides. It would be dangerous to get caught in the tunnels when the tide was coming in. If the surging waters didn't smash you on the structure, you could drown if you got caught without an air pocket.

"Hello, Mathew." a lady's voice said from behind him. Mathew just about jumped to the ceiling as he turned around to see who was talking, the kitchen knife he had taken up carrying drawn and ready to fight. He had heard no door or footsteps. The lady was floating in the air that explained the no footsteps. She was dressed in flames and shadows. "You asked, I am sending you help."

"Who are you?" Mathew was both amazed and terrified.

"I am ShadowDancer, an Ancient or a goddess as you humans like to call things. I am sending you someone who will help you get your family back together. She will be here in five days when your fathers ship arrives back."

"Five days may be too late, I heard them say they might get orders to execute." Mathew's love for his mom cast out his fear of ShadowDancer. She promised help, but it was his mom, and she was in danger.

"Do not be afraid, we will be there before any harm comes to your mom." she put a hand on his shoulder, "You have not been eating enough. You will need your strength when she arrives to help you."

"How will I know who you send?" Mathew seemed uncertain.

"Her eye will burn with fire from under her hood. Now go eat there is food to last you until it is time on the table and in the kitchen icebox that is also refilled with ice." ShadowDancer vanished before his eyes. He had heard a wizard could do things like that, but he had never seen it before.

*   *   *   *

*

Everyone had agreed to make Delmar and Peltricia the elders of the village. It took time for them to come up with a name. In the end they called the village Sein Estel or New Hope in elvish. Every family had a home and a shop of some kind. There were also buildings for town business and warehouses for storing everything they were producing. Even though they could harvest anything they needed from the land they still taught their children the trade skills that they knew. They also taught them how to defend their homes if they ever should have the need. Trade skills would help them blend in when they visited other town or societies, concealing their true source of sufficiency. Skills at defending themselves and their homes were just a practical part of living in their world.

Delmar walked out of the town hall with Peltricia, "We have had seven visitors now."

"Word will get out and we will have more." Peltricia smiled

"I just hope it was not a mistake opening the road." Delmar was concerned.

"We are respected here, and the road is not heavily traveled. I see nothing to worry about and it was the plan."

"I know, but we are self-sufficient and opening the doors could lead to trouble too."

"That is the isolationist elf in you. Tap into the human half a little more and go for the adventure." Peltricia laughed.

"You keep your optimism." Delmar could not help smiling when he looked at her, "I will keep training everyone to defend what we have."

Peltricia paused looking around, "You know I am surprised there was not already a settlement at this location. It is perfect with a natural source of water running through. Access was too easy to finish connecting to the road, almost like it was there once before and even the cut and level of the land."

Delmar looked at everything she was pointing out, "We have been living here for a short time. We have not had time yet to really look around. You may be right; we should see what we can dig up."

"I'll bring it up at our next town meeting." Peltricia vocalized her next thought, "I wonder if there was a settlement, what drove them away?"

*   *   *   *

*

The followers of ShadowDancer were many and scattered throughout the land. They did not necessarily advertise or promote converting anyone. They often smiled on the differences between people because they were different. She had helped them when nobody else would and told them to help others. For the most part that is what they did. In the south lands of the northern continent, some looked to Delmar as a leader, others looked to Samuel and others that did not look at leaders.

There was however a priestess, called upon by ShadowDancer to serve. For now at least there was one priestess and that was Terriala who was given the task to educate those followers of ShadowDancer that would listen. The first instruction of ShadowDancer was do not shed blood on an alter as a sacrifice to me. The second instruction was to help others.

Beyond these two things ShadowDancer had given no specific instructions to her people on things they must or must not do. Although ShadowDancer had given specific direction to others around the world these were not instructions for all her people.

Melina sister of Terriala was the only person ever sacrificed to ShadowDancer and out of respect for their sacrifice she accepted her as a messenger. There was much that Melina had seen and knew that she could not share with her still living sister. This did not affect the loyalty of either sister. As she sat in meditation by the statue of ShadowDancer Terriala heard Samuel approach. He stood in silence waiting for her to acknowledge him.

"What brings you here this evening?" she asked.

"Word has come back that Delmar and the followers with him have built a new village to the north. I was concerned their actions may bring the wrath of ShadowDancer." Samuel was filled with sincerity and pious passion.

"She has not told us how we must live or how to serve. Even we have built a tent city here with the time we have stayed. It has worked out well for those who leave and return. They go out and serve and help others and return and we help them. Helping each other is the best place to start helping others." Terriala patted the ground for him to come sit with her.

"That is all good, my priestess, but they are keeping warehouses of weapons and good and selling to those who pass by with need." Samuel's expression said he was sure he had made a very surprising and good point.

"Melina let us know that ShadowDancer was alright with the weapons and armor we have stored in the secret parts of the cave. Should she treat other followers different then she treats us?" Terriala paused. "Farmers and others pay wages for our help and we cause their lands to yield more abundant for them. Is this really so different then selling to them. Do you have any reports where they refused to help someone in need that did not have a means to pay?"

"You have corrected me on every thought." Samuel conceded.

"We can decide how to rule that which is ours to rule, like the order within our tent village. It is not our place to impose our ideals of what we think others should do for ShadowDancer. She has given us freedom to make choices, so every one of her followers chooses their own way. We need to accept that." Terriala leaned her head on Samuel's shoulder. "I know you care for our people, but we do not even begin to know all of her followers. There is no need for us to fight each other over matters she has not thought important enough to tell us what to do."

Samuel put an arm around her shoulder. "You are right. I am only exalting myself if I try to say what she wants when she has not told us."

Melina appeared in front of them, "Sister, Samuel, I bring a message for you both. I apologize for it being somewhat cryptic to you."

"It is an honor that you visit us sister Melina, messenger of ShadowDancer." Terriala bowed her head slightly.

"I do not have the privilege of an extended visit this time. Here is the message: ShadowDancer has sent her avatar out from her homeland. She had many stops but will be here in a short time."

"How will I know this avatar?"

"You will know her by the fire in her eyes." Melina faded quickly and was gone.

"What do we do to prepare for the coming of an avatar?" Samuel asked.

"I do not know, but I am sure we will know more as it gets closer. I didn't know she had an avatar." Terriala stood up. "It is time for our evening gathering. I will start by letting them know the good news."

*   *   *   *

*

The glimpses of Kelleeshia she got through windows on the way to the Magus were impressive. The building they were in was grandiose and ornately decorated. The presentation of the Magus was as ostentatious as the rest of the building. He was seated in what can only be described as a throne, overly ornate and gaudy. The room was designed to present an intimidating grandeur. Much of the effect was lost on Lyamy not having the same concept of materialistic value. She was impressed at the power and influence he had and starting to understand that the affluence of material wealth played a part in having power outside the savage continent.

As she approached, she bowed her head slightly acknowledging his authority in this place. "Greetings Magus Kremlern."

"Lyamy it is my honor." He gestured and his security and everyone else left the room. She was sure not far, but out of range of hearing normal conversation. "There is a lot of information that I need to share with you as instructed by the Ancient ShadowDancer. I normally look to her father the Ancient Eric Marland, but he supports her efforts also."

"I understand there is some urgency." She paused a moment. "Did you say father? Are they just another race born on Ethar with greater power?" From everything she knew and had seen in ShadowDancer's mind Lyamy trusted her still but was questioning the authority of one race to just rule over the rest.

The Magus stroked his beard before answering. "There is more to it than that. If you look back at your own history, there was a time when your races were made by the Ancients. Perhaps some time when we have more time, we can study the history and knowledge we have of the Ancients. Melina indicated you had a way of pulling information I want to give you from my mind."

Lyamy looked a little surprised but thought about what he said. "Well, I have had that kind of link with ShadowDancer, but she always initiated the link and pulled me into her mind. I should be able to open the link, but you will have to invite me in and push the information you want me to have. I don't know if I can do it with arcane magic only though."

The Magus smiled and held up his hand with the brass ring she had given him. The ring burst with a flame about six inches long and his eyes lit with the fire of the old magic. "I have felt the old magic, so you will not be violating anything using it to perform the link.”

“Good, then I think we can do this. Have you tried emulating things you do with arcane using the old magic?” Lyamy asked

“I have been experimenting.” He had an impish grin. “I am ready if you are.”

Lyamy placed her hand on his temple. She opened the link, and he invited her in. She tried to focus on the information he wanted to give her, but his mind was not as organized as ShadowDancer’s and she received a lot more then he intended on her knowing. She shook her head when they were done. “I am sorry, I saw much more then you meant to tell me. You have my word as an avatar your secrets are safe.”

“That was an awesome way to teach someone. You have my trust; I do not want to know what else you learned.” He looked perplexed. “How do you teach others if not like this.”

“You know I should have taught you this first.” She placed her hand on his temple again and pushed the knowledge to him, teaching him how to do exactly what she was doing to teach him.

“That is a lot more controlled.” The Magus looked her over with speculation working the gears behind his eyes. “You have enough power alone that I could not harness enough to challenge you. Whatever information you have gained, I really have no choice but to trust you. I find comfort in knowing we serve the same Ancients.”

He had given her the complete layout of Kelleeshia, with a quick study she knew where to go to take care of any business she needed in the city. She had gained his knowledge of maps and layout of places around Ethar, mostly the middle continent and northern continent. It seemed ShadowDancer did not want her getting lost. Then there were a series of missions. The information was available for her to look into but seemed to be set to rise up when needed also. She looked back at the Magus, "While your mind seems a bit, shall we say less then ordered, perhaps from my concept of an organized mind, you have done some interesting work with thought manipulation. You have set knowledge to triggers."

"Having knowledge set to trigger on events allows it to be dropped in a pool that cannot be read easily by mind readers, while readily available when I need it. A mind that is orderly like a file room allows anyone who finds a way in to have quick easy access to what they are looking for."

Lyamy looked at the light from the windows. "The sun is high, and I have to gather supplies. I will be back before sun falls to get the box that goes to ShadowKeep."

"There is no reason not to take it now." The Magus placed his hand on the arm of his chair and pressed a combination of gems. He pulled a box out of the compartment that opened. As he handed it to her, she could feel the life inside.

"Is this safe to store in an airless container?" Lyamy asked.

"That box can support the contents as long as it is needed. Yes, it is safe."

She slipped the box into her dimensional pocket, seemingly

making it vanish in thin air. "Then I will see you when I pass this way again."

The Magus had a puzzled look on his face, "I did not see the magic of your dimensional pocket, are you using yet another magic I do not know?"

She smiled. "I am the avatar of an ancient. I still have a few secrets."

"It is always a surprise and a delight to work with you." He sat down. "Would you mind telling the guard outside everyone can return now?"

"Of course." she gave her head a slight bow before turning and heading out the door.

Lyamy scrambled around the city gathering the things she was instructed to collect for each mission. She paused once with the intent of using her own ability to create the items needed and ShadowDancer appeared, informing her that she wanted to purchase the items to support the local economies. The sword she was about to buy would feed the blacksmiths family and he had made an open plea to the Ancients to help him. Lyamy asked if she should do business as her avatar or just as herself. She was told she could appear to those she helped as the avatar, but for general travel in town to go as herself so as not to draw too much attention. She let the shop owners know she was the avatar of ShadowDancer after making the purchases.

When she had left the gates of the city and was ready to start her run Lyamy took on the form of the avatar dressed only in flames and shadows. She liked the freedom the form offered. Then she altered time so that months of travel would pass in minutes of real time. Shadowkyn move naturally faster than most if not all other humanoid races when they are walking. Lyamy was given a gift of added speed so she moved more than twice as fast as other Shadowkyn. As a race they could naturally run fast, in excess of five times their walking speed and a sprint could double that. In short Lyamy could cover a lot of ground in a short period of time without altering time.

Very little time had passed when she reached the devastated path of the undead army. Life was slowly encroaching from the edges of dead area, new and fresh and young. At random plants were springing up where seeds had been blown even in the middle of the large area where necromancy took its toll. These were the tropics and with enough rain and sunshine, it was hard to keep the jungle down. Lyamy slowed down when she reached the first signs of bones and ash on the ground. She sniffed the air and followed the scent.

The three corpses were human. They looked young to her, but she was still not a good judge when it came to the ages of humans. They had been killed by swords, wider blades then her own. The wounds were from simple blades no magical qualities or residue. They had been stripped of weapons and valuables. Lyamy created a new hidden pocket just for the bodies. She used arcane magic to levitate and slide the bodies into the hidden pocket. The ground was marked with the pitting of the spilled blood making it clear the victims were from the Shadow Valley protected by ShadowKeep. With a wave of her hand, she scorched the ground turning the blood residue to ash.

Judging by the tracks there had been five assailants, also human or humanoid. Based on the size of the tracks and depth of the footprints she would guess they were wearing armor. They had made no attempt to hide their trail, so she followed with ease. As she approached, they appeared to be standing still until she shifted back to normal time.

"What are you doing in these parts?" she called from behind them.

The party of five stopped and turned around to face her. "What are you a fire elemental?" One asked.

"It is none of your business wench," another barked, "but if you must know we are here representing King Tagmerian claiming salvage rights to this land for Ehrbron."

"These are free lands, does your claim give you authority to kill others trying to find profit in adventure and hard work?" Lyamy's eyes were glowing with flames, an effect that may have been lost being clothed in flames, but she could feel the old magic rising within.

"She knows about the other three." one of them whispered.

"Shut up!" another snapped.

"You can submit to our authority and hand over any treasure you have found or follow their fate." What appeared to be the leader of the group snapped pulling his sword and positioning his shield.

Lyamy pulled her swords, "You each have one chance right now to submit to arrest and be taken before the law in ShadowKeep or die. If you chose to live and face trial lay on your belly."

The other four pulled their weapons and started towards her. They hesitated ever so slightly when her swords burst into flames but continued towards her. When they were withing seven feet they suddenly rushed forwards. The middle two attempting to thrust swords forwards lifting their shields with the intent to block any counterattack. The outer two attempted to flank both sides swinging their swords where her back should have been.

Lyamy went into the air as they rushed flipping over them. Her blades moved so fast they appeared to turn into a sheet of flames as shoulder height. She landed on her feet behind them facing their backs. They almost seemed unaffected for a moment, then the bodies collapsed, and the heads rolled off. The flames seared as they cut making it bloodless and unrealistic.

She turned to face their leader. He held his shield high and started backing away. "Your men are dead, and you cower and do not stand for their honor and loyalty to you?" Lyamy was angry but resisted killing what she felt was a coward. "Drop your shield and put up your sword." She sheathed her swords and they vanished. He dropped his shield and sheathed his sword. "You cannot move faster than I can cut you up. You will receive the marks of shame for lacking the honor to die with your men."

"But" She moved before he could finish his objection one slice with each claw on her right hand leaving a lopsided pentagram on his left cheek. From eye to ear, ear to jaw, the length of his jaw to his mouth, from the corner of his eye to his nose and the last one crossing the two to his nose and mouth. They would form a permanent scar.

She began the ritual of bonding him to her licking the blood from each claw in front of him. "With your blood I bond you to my will." she felt a piece of his spirit taken into her, the rush of power and the sweet savor. "You are mine to do as I will."

He went gaunt, "As you will, Master." Feeling her power over him.

The old magic was powerful, the bond was almost permanent. "You will gather all the loot you have collected from these fields and from the people you killed and give it to me now."

"As you command." he collected everything from his men and his own belongings. Lyamy put it all in a hidden pocket as he gave it to her.

"Now you will haul the remains of your men back to your king and tell him by order of the avatar of ShadowDancer the armies of Ehrbron are forbidden to set foot in these lands or claim any salvage. Tell him even as he bears the scars of his dream, he is writing his own fall from power."

"I shall deliver your message." He gathered his men, using the materials from their tents to form a makeshift litter. He harnessed it to his shoulders and started southward.

Lyamy altered time and headed to ShadowKeep.

*   *   *   *

*

HonorLord, Hans Spardic, the High Lord of ShadowKeep knew Lyamy was coming. ShadowDancer told him she was sending her avatar. He was also one of the Ancients that were inheriting the world of Ethar. He had been appointed as High Lord of ShadowKeep just before the last war after the earthquake that split the world killed the rest of the leadership from ShadowKeep. Darvarias his son helped him rule along with the council and the civilian government from Shadow Valley. Like ShadowDancer, his son also inherited the abilities of an Ancient, along with the magics of his mother.

Hans had come to Ethar with Eric and Bonny and the three of them were the beginning of what was called the new Ancients. Eric had saved the life of an Elven princess and she wound up having his child after she married the crowned prince of the City of Talmorg. That child became ShadowDancer. Darvarias was the son of Hans and his wife Stralina a Jinni who died at the beginning of the recent war. These two children were the first of the next generation of the new Ancients, similar to the gods and goddesses of myth on earth. Hans was the Ancient of war. Darvarias toyed with his abilities, but there was no clearly defined roll he was playing. He care for the peoples of Shadow Valley and responded to others throughout the world, although not as actively as ShadowDancer. He also did not have any alter ego name, or title; he was known by his name Darvarias.

Hans and L'Akyra were not married although she had taken up living with him most of the time anyway. She was from another dimension, neither from the one they were in now on the world of Ethar, nor from the dimension he came from when he left earth. A chance meeting fated them together, but they were not settled on the virtue of getting married after previous mishaps. She still operated as his right hand when she was around. She had been good for him and helped him deal with his losses. She helped him control the darkness that had seeped into his soul. She had stopped him from destroying the sword he was known for carrying when she found the inscriptions hidden in the handle. It was not just a spirit stealer; it gave him command of the armies of the dead when he summoned them. He was still contemplating destroying the weapon and freeing the spirits to move on.

The Avatar of ShadowDancer was bringing a package. He knew what it contained and would be there when it was opened to preside over the event. It was an event with an outcome that had not been predetermined. He would make sure if it did not go in her favor, she would not know what she missed. If things did go in her favor, he would be privileged to see to her reward and provide her with instruction.

There were only two ways into ShadowKeep and Shadow Valley. You could fly in over the top of the ring of high mountains and parapets or the keep. This approach was guarded by dragons, friends and protectors. You could come in the front gates. The road to the front gates zigzagged across the face of the cliffs that were a part of the mountain face the gates were built in. There was no cover or hiding places for miles out from the base of the mountain. As far as the world knew these were the only ways in and out other than magic. HonorLord knew an Avatar of

ShadowDancer would have little difficulty slipping passed all of their defenses. Fortunately, he had no reason not to trust anyone ShadowDancer was sending to him.

Drakalon was an older dragon, much older than most. He had told HonorLord once that he was there when they first came to Ethar. Of course, that means Drakalon was one of the old ones who carved the course of events before the Ancients and spurned them to power. As HonorLord stepped out onto the top of the wall from the stair Drakalon shifted from dragon to his human form and greeted him. "Greetings HonorLord, High Lord of ShadowKeep, and friend of the ages."

"Greetings my friend, Drakalon, old one from times forgotten."

"You are troubled."

"Indeed." HonorLord looked along the precipices that stretched in either direction. "I am the Ancient of war, and yet I do not accept death easily. I even find killing to be worse than accidental death or the course of time. There is a great contradiction within me."

"A piece of clay is neither good nor evil. Even the form it takes does not make it evil, a rock is a rock, and a cup is a cup. It takes decisions to become good or evil. I have seen no race that is clearly or easily defined as either."

"I killed enemies, stopping time and made it appears as though they killed each other. I felt the darkness as if touched by evil for what I did and yet saved thousands of lives."

Drakalon laughed, "Something inside of you said you did wrong, cheated, didn't play fair, maybe changed the course of events causing results that should not have happened. It is easy when you see a little girl to tell yourself killing her for no reason is evil. Maybe not as easy to tell yourself killing an enemy who is trying to kill you is good and even if you learn they were just trying to defend that same little girl you feel justified in defending yourself was not evil. And yet you acted against an enemy you know was attacking for no reason other than power and you feel guilty because some part of you says it was not honorable, though they would not have hesitated to do the same to you. Perhaps good and evil are concepts that cannot be so clearly defined?"

"To have the experience and memories you have spanning the millenniums, perhaps I could see more clearly the lines of good and evil."

"You can you know. You are an Ancient and I could share with you all my memories." Drakalon moved in front of him, "But know this first. Memories do not make choices or decisions, only you do, and in the end, knowledge can cloud clear thinking and does not replace your own experience. I will gladly pass to you all that is in my memories, the time will come when someone will have to stand in my place. If you accept, I will choose you now so you can be prepared when that time eventually comes."

"I accept, and perhaps there will be time to also learn understanding from your experience."

Drakalon placed his hand on HonorLord's temple, time shifted as the moment was captured. "Enter into my mind and when we are done you will have a library of all I know."

HonorLord slipped in, Drakalon hid nothing from him. The volume was more than his human brain could have handled, but he was an Ancient, no longer restricted to the finite capacity of mortality. The sharing seemed to take forever in an instant and it was done. "You once let the darkness overwhelm you convinced you were evil?" HonorLord realized that was the same path he was considering although he had not gone that far. "Perhaps it is good I learn from you before I am overcome."

"The cycle of death and darkness are part of life and time. A small seedling sprouts and it is full of life. It grows and the life in the middle dies becoming the hard fiber that gives it strength to stand. The bigger and stronger it grows the more it depends on what is dead to give it strength as it becomes a tree. The mightiest tree in the forest is protected by a shield of dead bark with a thin layer of soft pliable life wrapped around a massive core of dead wood. Life depends upon death to nurture growth." Drakalon returned them to the normal flow of time.

"That seems like a rather morbid way to look at the cycle of life" HonorLord realized the entire life of Drakalon was in his mind like a library he could easily pull knowledge from. "I have to admit you are right about at least one thing life does seem to be a thin skin standing upon that which is not living."

"You are a man or were a man born of two parents, born of a generation before them and back for how many generations? If they all still lived, would there be room enough for you to live? Or perhaps there are many ways you depend on death to live? How many plants and animals have died so you can eat or have a home."

"I will hold onto the thought as part of the cycle of life." HonorLord laughed.

"And that is why you feel guilty and has a sense of darkness from killing twelve enemies that would have happily killed you. You are not a necromancer, yet you carry the sword of one."

"You are the one who warred against Keltoe, the oldest of the dragons who came to this world. Instead of destroying you he delivered you from the darkness within. Perhaps I feel guilty because I may have been able to do the same for those necromancers instead of killing them?"

"Deeds done you can reflect on and gain understanding and wisdom. You can even have regret or remorse. They are done and you cannot go back and change them, so unless you want the darkness to overwhelm you, you must separate yourself from the events and hold tight to the core beliefs that make you who you are."

"She is here." HonorLord glanced down through the stone in the direction of Lyamy. "I meant to tell you, the avatar of ShadowDancer is coming and now is here. I need you to share witness to the opening of the box she is bringing, er brought." he started to step away and turned back, "We will be back shortly." He turned the rest of the way and ran down the stairwells to the keep below. She was waiting for him in the throne room.

Lyamy felt him coming and knew he was an Ancient. As he stepped into the room, she dropped to one knee and bowed her head slightly in his direction as he walked over to her. "Greetings HonorLord, high lord of ShadowKeep, Ancient of War. I sense you have smiled on me before."

"Arise Lyamy, Avatar of ShadowDancer, of the leopard clan, champion of the Shadowkyn."

She stood as instructed. "I ask your audience on three matters: One the disposition of the bodies of citizens of Shadow Valley slain by southern kingdom soldiers of Ehrbron salvaging in the wake of the undead armies. Two dealings with the soldiers that committed the crime. And Three a delivery I was to make to you in person."

"What bodies?" HonorLord inquired.

"I have them with me in a hidden pocket and will deliver them where you instruct." she answered. "There was no justification for their death. They were slain by soldiers of the southern kingdom without warning as part of a claim by Ehrbron to salvage rights to anything of value left by the war."

HonorLord waved a guard over and gave him instructions. The guard took off. "I would see who has been slain and have their families claim them. Ehrbron has no right to claim anything from a war in which they were defeated. The kingdom will be held accountable in addition to the men who committed such a crime against civilians."

"You are not of this world." Lyamy looked hard at HonorLord, then quickly apologized. "I am sorry, it is not my place to take notice of such things."

"There is no harm in seeing the truth. I will not ask how you knew." HonorLord laughed. "I am what I am. Where I came from, I was Jaffro Jamis, when I was brought to Ethar I was known as Hans Spardic the Ebony Warrior because of my black armor and now I am HonorLord. Now tell me about these soldiers of Ehrbron."

"When I challenged them there were five and all, but their leader attacked me. So, four lost their heads and their leader cowered. I called him a coward for not fighting with his men and took control of him like I would a beast to bring it to my command. He will do anything I tell him to do, and I can use him to see events around him. If I choose, I can take control of his being and do things directly using his body. I stripped the soldiers and took everything he had short of what he needs as a soldier heading home. I instructed him to take the bodies to his king and let him know that Ehrbron is forbidden to lay any claim to any salvaging in the lands north of the southern kingdoms. I told him to tell the king '*Tell him even as he bears the scars of his dream, he is writing his own fall from power*.' I sent him back to Ehrbron."

"I see you have been touched by ShadowDancer and see glimpses of the future." HonorLord walked over and sat down in his throne. "I will wait on acting against Ehrbron to see the results of your work. I will honor your command against Ehrbron doing any salvaging. I was told you find a way to get things done without killing if you can. Where you hasty in killing the soldiers?"

"They were wielding weapons attempting to strike me down. I

could have done many things, but there is a time for all things. I cannot always send attackers back naked, I will get a reputation as a safe enemy to make. ShadowDancer did not give me the power and skills so I could hide them in a box. I cannot have the world look upon her avatar as soft."

"I do not disagree. The fact that you defend your actions means you still have a conscience concerning these matters." HonorLord stood, walked over to her and patted her shoulder.

Several guards came in and laid tarps out on the floor. Lyamy knew what they were for and levitated the corpses out of her hidden pocket and placed them on the tarps. "That is all of them. To me it looks like they were deliberately injured before killing. There was no sign they fought back."

"There is darkness in those kingdoms, but not everyone is party to the darkness. I cannot just wipe them out, not even their armies. That small group earned what you did to them. There are others even in the army that are not evil and would not have participated in such a vile act."

"I saw that when we sent the armies away from the sanctuary." Lyamy had realized some of those soldiers were only there because their families needed to eat. "I need to head to Ehrbron, when I am done here to help some of those who are not evil."

"Let us go up and meet the dragons so you can open this box for me and they can witness." HonorLord lead Lyamy up to meet Drakalon. They climbed quickly, but not running up the many tiers of spiral stairs.

"You really have dragons here or is that a reference you use for something else." Lyamy asked as she followed. She got her answer as they stepped out onto the parapets before he could answer. She saw dozens at a glance and tried not to stare at them. "I have never seen dragons before." The beasts were massive, but she showed no fear, she had ridden on the back of a horvalka that was bigger then the beast she touched.

"This one is brave, HonorLord." Drakalon bellowed as she touched him. He looked at Lyamy, "You must be the avatar of ShadowDancer, I am Drakalon, what is your name child?"

She looked up into his eyes. She could see flames behind the eyes that suggested greater power than the normal eyes could see. "Forgive me, I am new to dragons. I am Lyamy. It is an honor to meet you." She brought the fires to her eyes, both old magic and ancient, then drew them back. "I have passed being a child and even an apprentice for that matter." she explained trying not to be disrespectful while correcting him.

"I have seen thousands of years go by, "Drakalon bellowed with laughter, "I meant no offense, but to me you are still very young. She has spirit and youth, but I perceive in her she has more years than she has on the outside. Perhaps we should get to the business that brought you up here?"

"Indeed." HonorLord stepped up to the two of them. "Lyamy place the box on the ground between the three of us."

Lyamy did as she was instructed. "The box is very pretty, with the gold and gems that cover it, but do they serve a purpose?"

HonorLord answered, "In this case yes, the gold carving of a dragon is symbolic of what is in the box and the gems are configured to enable the box to carry something much bigger then the box itself. Now carefully open the box and stand back in the circle."

Lyamy unfastened the latches and opened the box. Light emanated from the container as it opened. And was like sunbeams coming out as the box was fully open and Lyamy stepped back. A golden dragon formed in the light, no taller than she was. It turned looking at each of them. It stopped facing Lyamy, dipped his head down and rolled it from side to side as if clearing the any stiffness away and stretched his wings to a span of about twenty-five feet. "Link with me avatar and I shall come to your aid when you call upon me. I can fly you and a companion around maybe two depending on their size. I will be able to do more as I grow."

She looked at him for a moment, then put out a claw to draw a few drops of blood. "Are you sure?"

He read her intent and laughed, "You do not need blood to make a bond with the magic you are calling the magic of the Ancients. It is a bond of sharing not one of us dominating the other." He was a golden dragon, with four legs and two wings. He held out his left front foot, as much a hand as a foot, with dragon claws and all. "Place your left hand in mine. My name is Pterdin."

She did as he asked. There was a buildup of power in their touch, she felt the spirit of the dragon touching hers. She gently pushed back a little and they seemed to mix, becoming one as touching. It felt as though they both gained something without losing anything. She studied what happened. It was a willing bond from both parties without domination of control given to one party. "I like this better. There is a burden with a bond for both parties if one has dominance or control." She stumbled a little on her thoughts and added, "Not that other bonds are bad, just I like this better."

"I see why you are chosen." Pterdin articulated, "We are chosen to work together. I am your mount and companion. I understand you do not use a mount on the ground because you move faster without one. I can carry you in the air even across the oceans. I will also come to your help in battle if you need me."

"You are not sent by ShadowDancer, you are from the old one?" She turned to Drakalon, "You are one of the old ones. I am honored by both of you and accept you as a companion, friend and I perceive you also serve to watch me if I get out of control? I can accept that. I have not been given limits and it will be good to have someone who will warn me if I am overstepping what I should do."

"You are perceptive." Drakalon stated. "Be aware that you are touched by ShadowDancer's ability to glimpse into the future. Future events are not absolute, and your perception gives you the ability to sometimes change what might happen. Just like this it will give you a greater understanding of everything around you. It can also give you conflicting perceptions around events that are a major nexus to things ahead. Pterdin is not there to stop you from doing anything. We chose not to rule here anymore a long time ago. We now only advise and help when asked. You Lyamy are a fulcrum of change. All of the old ones will be observing you for signs of our role in the future of Ethar."

Lyamy contemplated what he was say. "So, you are telling me that concerning events at least for now the world revolves around me. Choices and mistakes, I make are effecting the future of the entire world?"

HonorLord let a laugh slip out before suppressing the rest. "I apologize for laughing, it has to do with what you said and where I am from." He started to explain. "Never mind, it would take too much to explain and has nothing to do with what is actually happening now."

Drakalon paused looking at HonorLord and then back to Lyamy. "To a certain extent yes. You are not the only focus point of change, but you are one."

Lyamy looked down at the box she had delivered. The box was still decorated with the gems, but the golden dragon that was on the cover was gone. "Do I keep that box?"

"If you want to. I have no use for it." The large dragon stretched out a wing. "I have been a witness, Lyamy has been accepted as worthy by her companion."

It was not until Drakalon had stood up on his hind legs and stretched that Lyamy realized he was much bigger than her giant horvalka back home. "And if I had not been worthy?"

"You would have never known." HonorLord answered. "Pterdin, can you form shift yet?"

Pterdin took on a human form, "Apparently I can." His hair was a golden blond his skin held a golden tan, Pterdin's human form was one of physical stature and prowess.

HonorLord stared towards the stairwell entry, "We shall have a celebration and I will introduce you as ShadowDancer's avatar at a dinner banquet. You should probably make the appearance in the proper attire."

With a thought Lyamy was dressed in shadows and flames representing her ancient. They went down returning the throne room. Lyamy noticed that ShadowKeep was prepared for a celebration welcoming her. After HonorLord took care of some formal business, he escorted her to Shadow Valley in the protective circle of mountains guarded by ShadowKeep. The area covered by the valley as they stepped out of the back entrance to ShadowKeep was much larger than the outside of the ring of mountains protecting it. Supplementing her vision with the different layers of magical true vision she studied the magic that formed the valley. It was the working of one of the Ancients, an overlapping of dimensions allowing the valley to expand as much as it needed to be ignoring what would otherwise have been the natural limits in size.

There were other workings in place too. Magic that effected the people who lived here. There were also the effects of powers she could not see. Part of her already knew there had to be more layers of power then what she could use, but the gaps supported by unseen threads confirmed her suspicions beyond anything she had previously seen. She had asked Pterdin about it and he informed her that there are seven sources of power that most of the Ancients knew about and used. There were several more sources that the old ones or oldest dragons knew about some they used and some they did not dare touch.

Pterdin seemed willing to give her any information he had. She learned that just over twenty years ago three strangers came to this world and it was discovered afterward that they were counted among the Ancients. One of them was ShadowDancer's father, Eric, then there was his wife now, not at the time, Bonny and HonorLord or Hans Spardic. Lyamy did not ask too many questions and changed the subject after she learned that Bonny was not ShadowDancer's mother, but an elven queen, who was a princess at the time. From what Lyamy understood other races put different emphasis on marriage and children then the Shadowkyn and this all sounded like something they would not approve of. With Shadowkyn your parents were the adults of your den, it did not matter who spawned you.

There was a gathering in the open field waiting for their arrival and the people seemed happy to see her. These were HonorLord's people, and she respected that. She was amazed at how they celebrate her presence and gave respect to ShadowDancer. It seems the Ancients do not compete for followers and did not mind sharing the adoration. HonorLord introduced Lyamy to the gathering with a very nicely worded speech, obviously planned. She returned some platitudes and answered a few questions from the gathered celebration. Lyamy sensed this was all prepared and planned ahead, perhaps even the questions were handpicked from a survey.

Back inside the Keep there was a banquet that lasted a few hours in her honor. There were more speeches, some honoring her, some talking

about relations between ShadowKeep and the communities on the Savage

continent. ShadowDancer made a showing, made a speech and ate at

the main table. She more quietly informed Lyamy this was all formality

and fluff that the other races do to build friendships between different

communities. "Just put your best foot forward, relax and enjoy what you

can." she had said.

When everyone had gone for the night, Lyamy use the gift

ShadowDancer had given her and blinked to get a full night rest. She

climbed back up to the parapets and began her routine forms practice.

Practice helped her stay fit and keep her training fresh. She found it helped

her clear her thinking also. After her first hour she heard something move

in the shadows and realized she was not alone and had not checked before

she started.

"You are smooth and well-practiced." Drakalon stepped out of the

shadows. He shifted and changed transformed in this human appearance.

"You have been through a lot of training."

"ShadowDancer provided my trainers." She did not miss a step in

her routine, "Perhaps you have more training or tips you can offer?"

Drakalon laughed, "Have you tried riding the flow of time with

your actions?"

She stopped what she was doing and gave him a bow of her head

like a student to their master. "That does not sound familiar. I would

be honored if you could show me what you are talking about. I see the threads of magic and time but have not used this in flow with combat training."

"Take a ready stance we will do some sparring." He also took a stance facing her. "Now watch the flow of the time threads and my movement." He tapped her on the shoulder easily avoiding her attempt to block.

Lyamy watched and saw how he was attaching his motion to the flow of the time threads, "So I can counter by also riding the threads, Like this." His next strike missed as she tapped his shoulder. They sparred back and forth for several minutes.

"You picked this up quickly." Drakalon noted. "You can ride all aspects of combat on the flow of the time threads."

"If both sides in a fight ride the flow of time threads, are they just conceding to the fate of events allowing the threads of time to determine the outcome?"

He moved at her again and she dodged, "I suppose you could look at it that way, but if you do not follow the threads you give the advantage to the opponent who is."

As they came at each other again she asked, "What about this?" Lyamy bent the threads of time he was following, and he landed on the ground next to her.

Getting back up, "I suppose that is an option too." he stepped back. "You are indeed avatar of ShadowDancer. Time is not fixed for you. You have picked up some of her ability to lord over time a quasi-dimension.

There are things that even the old ones cannot do. Have you had any other time related events?”

“Not me, but a friend that I accidentally killed and ShadowDancer brought back from beyond sleep has random visions of future events as though they had already happened. She refers to the future events as if they are past.” Lyamy got a concerned look, “She is not aware when these things happen to her, that is not going to happen to me is it?”

“No.” Drakalon was obviously being serious. “You have control of what you do. ShadowDancer is the daughter of the ancient of the new order, Eric.”

“Pterdin has told me this much. I stopped pursuing my curiosity when the relationships went places, I would not have expected from human or elf races.”

“We dragons came here a very long time ago. This world was raw material and undeveloped. We had visions of doing such a better job of bringing a world to life then what had happened on our home world. We really did no better, but even since we conceded to our shortcoming, we have made an effort to guide the world towards better ideals. Most of us have. It seems there were a few among us who had no intent of making a peaceful world to start with. With all said and done, they were right about one thing; Conflict promotes growth.”

“And this has to do with me, ShadowDancer and altering time how?” Lyamy felt a little tense about what he may be leading to.

Eric descended from Gaharias, a lost lineage from earth came to

Ethar with more power than any of the ancients has ever had before and gained yet more power in the process of doing good. We suspect he alone has more power than the combined power of the old ones. We think that is where ShadowDancer has gotten her ability to see the future and effect events along the time-line. This is a very dangerous power and one that needs to be used with extreme caution."

Lyamy thought carefully about what he was saying. "So, since I have this power, I am a threat to everyone with the potential of accidentally altering the course of history. Is there anyone who can teach me how to use and control this power?"

Drakalon relaxed as if having told her took weight off his mind. "As far as I know you are one of only three who have this ability. Of the three, Eric has not used it that we are aware of, ShadowDancer is still as new to this as you are and then there is you." Drakalon paused. "You are disciplined, and you have found the ability to maintain control over the other magic you possess, including the hunger of the old magic. It is in your hands to use caution and exercise control in testing what you can and cannot do."

"So, you suggest I experiment with it. This is not like having a new power source and testing the application of used with already know magic. Are you saying I can move forward and back in time? And do you mean shifting back in time to ten minutes ago or actually going back in time ten minutes so there are two of me? I get that by seeing future events I can alter the future by changing what is happening now, but are you saying I can alter the past also and change what has already happened now?"

"I am saying maybe, but only the three of you will ever be able to answer those questions. This is why the old ones observe and watch you to see what our future roles will be. Our world is changing, or should I say your world is changing and it may be our time to move on again and let go of the bonds we have had here. You are a part of the new powers that have been chosen to operate here by intelligent forces more powerful than ourselves."

Lyamy was trying to get a grasp on what he was telling her. In her mind she took the time thread that was hers and twisted a single tiny loop pulling the future thread to form the loop. She looked and there was another of her standing next to her looking back. Then she felt herself pulled back and looked at her past self that just pulled the thread. She had not used the old magic source, and she had not used the magic source she referred to as the Ancient's magic source. She had used another source she did not know was there until she used it. Like the other sources of magical power, once you know it is there, it is everywhere and hard to believe you didn't see it before. This source was dark like threads of dark shadow. It felt like a source she should not know was there, a dark glue that held things together. "What source is this I have touched on? Dark threads of power."

Drakalon had seen the double pulled out of time and the loop as she vanished backwards. "So you can time loop." He looked at her and she could sense he was looking at her through many layers of magic. "I can not see these dark threads you speak of, but from your reaction, I would guess you have touched on a source that we have referred to as a forbidden source." Lyamy noted Drakalon seemed a little shaken.

Lyamy sat down. She looked at Drakalon. "I have gone from being an apprentice being disciplined for spying on my leader to a champion for my people, then an avatar for ShadowDancer and now I learn I am in possession of a power that could threaten everything and everyone if I make a mistake. I have family too. With totally phenomenal power, my family is very important, but as long as I stay with them, the offspring of our den all have access to what I know to learn and develop as they grow. I barely trust myself with what I know. I need to know how to spare our children the danger of having this knowledge."

"I know how I lock away knowledge in my own mind, but I do not have a bond that allows others to access what I know unless I give them temporary access to specific information." Drakalon pondered. "You should ask ShadowDancer. She has granted you power and I think you have learned more then she expected."

"Thank you Drakalon. I appreciate the wisdom or your experience you offer me in consultation. ShadowDancer has never taken back anything she has given, but I would see the wisdom if she took this back. I will find a private place and consult with ShadowDancer." Lyamy stood and headed for the stairwell.

"Good fortune, Lyamy." Drakalon said as she started down the stairs before the door closed behind her. He knew this Avatar had more power than most Ancients, which was small compared to that of ShadowDancer and Darvarias and they had less power than Eric, Bonny, and Hans.

Lyamy came out of the stairwell at the main floor level and wandered for a while until she stumbled upon the fountain garden courtyard. It was quiet and peaceful. She sat down and called upon ShadowDancer. Within moments her goddess appeared, Lyamy had come to accept calling ShadowDancer a goddess. It was simpler to say and did not have the connotation of being very old. The two of them sat together and talked for hours. Lyamy shared everything she knew and could do including her conversation with Drakalon. ShadowDancer smiled at her and told her she was only twenty-one now herself and when she was thirteen her powers started to become apparent. At first, she had no one to teach her what was happening until her father asked her. Then he would teach her what he could, but at that time he was still relatively new to what he had also.

A few things that ShadowDancer said stood out to her and did help her become more comfortable with what she knew and could do. "You are my Avatar, you can do almost anything I can do, but take your time learning, you can only make mistakes with what you do." She had explained that having a power does not make you a threat, being willing to use it without thinking does. ShadowDancer also said she would make mistakes, but to do good you cannot let that stop you from taking action.

Lyamy was much calmer and accepting her position. "How do you know I was the right choice? I come from a race that writes their history in blood and brutal savagery. Those soldiers I killed the other day, I had no thought of mercy and they had no chance against me. I saw them as a message to their king and country. Are you sure I am not a mistake?"

ShadowDancer smiled and put an arm around her shoulder. "The fact that you are willing to question yourself confirms you have a conscience that will keep you in balance. You are not a mistake. Remember I told you once I will not make a new "Ancient" by mistake. I have glimpses of the future and in every glimpse where the future is good, you are there as part of my council. I am certain you belong. As for your worries about what the children of your den might learn, do not worry. Your mind was expanded so that you could hold and handle the knowledge you have and the magics you can manipulate. Your children have not had this done. They will learn and they will all learn different things, but none will learn so much as to have the overwhelming power you do. They will each have their own schools of knowledge."

"What about these dark shadow threads?" Lyamy asked.

"I see them too." ShadowDancer stated, "Like with everything else, use all magic with caution. There are seven sources of magic that most of the Ancients use and who knows how many more there might be. You know three of the seven actually four if you thought about it. You know arcane, primordial, alaquine the blue fire and if you thought about it you would realize you also know divine which you use for healing, protection and some other things. I would say you have seen and maybe even used elemental magic perhaps thinking it was an extension of arcane. You have, but without training used psionic power, by many not considered a magic and while used by the Ancients, not counted as a magic to them either. You have yet to discover vesper which does a balancing of dark and light forces that are more like waves then threads. Then there is barrier magic. Barrier magic is an intelligent source, and you can only use this source if one or more of the barriers between dimensions has accepted you to be trusted. Like your companion Pterdin accepts you and now you can call upon him and he will serve your needs but is free to change his mind should you violate that trust, so it is with the barriers."

"So, you don't have a name for the magic of the dark shadow threads?" Lyamy reworded her question.

"I do not, what should we call that source? Dark thread magic works for me, what do you think."

"Unless we should discover something else, like what it calls itself." Lyamy agreed. Her power was not being taken away. She was going to be on ShadowDancer's Council of Ancients, but she already knew this from her own glimpses of the future.

"We need to equip our people to effectively defend themselves." Samuel was insistent with Terriala. "We have had three different parties now attacked while traveling to different towns to help with their fields, or other work that the townsfolk needed help with."

"I agree, but not the weapons from the cave. We have money, our people have money and part of helping the communities is to purchase what we can and help their business. We want people to see our coins and know we are a part of their economies." Terriala was weary of the argument. "The idea is for communities to want to welcome our people and for half breeds and outcasts to have a place in the existing societies. If we isolate all our business to ourselves, we are no different than those who would have us isolated from their societies."

Samuel pointed to her waist. "You carry the weapons you crafted."

"Yes, and I crafted them. For those who can craft their own let them." Terriala was finished. "As priestess I will tell our people how they can serve our goddess, then as their leader you can tell them anything you want. This is not by order of ShadowDancer, but what I say is in compliance with what she has directed us. If you choose to contradict me you can answer if we are asked, but access to that which is for service to the goddess shall be held back for real defense should our people come under attack."

"We have not been questioned on anything we have done so far. I am confident we will not be faced with trouble for creating our own defenses." Samuel started to rant out of her tent.

"Maybe this is why her avatar is coming?" Terriala asked before the tent flap closed. "Give me guidance ShadowDancer please."

"You are correct." Melina stated as she appeared. "It is for the good of our people and those in the lands they touch to do business with merchants when possible. ShadowDancer wants her people in this part of the world armed and prepared to defend each other and the townships and people if needed. It is also true that ShadowDancer wants to leave that as a choice. It is acceptable to distribute one sword per follower to the people that you have crafted. This will provide them an immediate defense and ability to defend each other."

"So, Samuel is right too." Terriala stated.

"There is something for you to do before you distribute the sword though. Create whatever blade you wish on the ground in front of you. Then place your hand on the blade. Push your holy power into the blade and whisper Holy Blade."

Terriala did as instructed. Then picked the blade up. "Now what?"

"Hold it out and will it to activate." Melina smiled when the blade was engulfed in a golden flame. "Now you can cast that permanently on any blade you want. It is a holy enchantment so intent will determine how it behaves. If an enemy picks up this blade with the intent of doing harm to our people, the sword will burn their hand. Forcing them to drop it."

"I would that I had a clear understanding of ShadowDancer's will and a means of presenting it better to her people." Terriala sighed.

"You are doing well, sister. Just remember our people need to do things for themselves also and have fun. Have a seasonal festival. Most harvesting is done for the year, when the last teams come home from the final harvesting have a big party."

"Thank you Melina. What can you tell me about our avatar?"

"She comes from the savage continent." Melina was like a little girl sharing secrets all smiles and excited. "She is one of the cat people and she is very powerful. She is also very pretty although very different in looks then us. Her ways are very different from ours also."

"Cat people? Do they have fur, how different are they?"

"They are like humanoid cats, mostly they don't have fur, although she still had a beautiful leopard pattern in her skin coloration and there is a stripe of fur down her back and to the tip of her tail. I guess she has a few other hereditary fur patches, but for the most part smooth skin. They are funny too; they didn't understand how a female could feed their litter with only two until they learned we normally only have one child born at a time."

"She is a cat that stands upright. What about her face?" Terriala was intrigued and anxious now to meet this avatar.

"Her face is closer to ours then a cat,but she still has some viscous teeth if she shows them and really cute cat ears. She has retractable claws on her fingers and toes also. They are not so different as eftites, they can breed with other races."

"I guess I will know now when I see her." Terriala smiled.

"It is good to spend a few minutes with you, sister." Melina gave her a hug. "I must return to ShadowDancer."

"Yes, it is always good when we have a few minutes." Terriala watched her fade. Terriala began drawing swords from the ground and blessing them with holy sword in groups of ten. She would have them ready for the evening gathering. She was not happy that Samuel had

48

argued the matter with her and she would let him brood until the meeting, although if he had not argued she might not have asked. She decided she would have to spend more time asking for guidance instead of trying to figure out what she thought ShadowDancer would want. It was that very thing, individuals deciding what their goddess wanted instead of finding out from the source that was already causing division in their people.

It did not take her long to have all the swords she needed for this evening gathering. There were normally about one hundred fifty people at their evening meetings. She created and enchanted two hundred, if she came up short, those that are always here she would take care of after the gathering. Word would get out and others would come by and visit to get their gifts later and she would take care of them as they arrived. This was not the first magic she had learned from ShadowDancer or Melina. She had learned to apply Divine power in many ways, including a hidden carrying bag that opened into a different dimension giving her a place to carry things and not be affected by the weight. She levitated the swords into the hidden bag and stepped out of her tent.

She was wearing her priestess clothing. In appearance it was very scant made in a way that to some extent emulated ShadowDancer's appearance, but it provided protection from all weather. She had several of the same outfit, but there was nothing she had found she could not do with the outfit on so far. The material did not seem to take damage for that matter the outfit seemed to have inherent qualities of heavy armor with no encumbrance. She was not intended to be a warrior, but obviously

ShadowDancer wanted her protected.

Terriala walked out into the glade where they had their gatherings. She looked out where seats and tables had been grown up from the ground, some living wood, some stone. The followers who were present brought food and shared as they did every evening. A hush spread outward as they saw her walk to the lectern. She started by expressing her hopes that everyone had a day with memories to make them all happy. Then she reviewed the only two rules ShadowDancer had given them as her followers. Then she followed that with praise and thanks for the things they had received.

"We are all different from the peoples we came from and different from each other." Terriala emphasized. "Variety gives us strength. Each of us chooses our own path, how and when we help others and when we help ourselves. The harvest season is near a close and when the last of our people return home it is time for us to celebrate together and separately. We will set aside a time to celebrate as a people and have fun as individuals. Samuel has pointed out to me we need to protect ourselves from random assaults by brigand and other dangers that confront us when we travel from place to place." She noted Samuel shifting uneasy where he sat. "I brought his request to ShadowDancer and while we buy things from the community markets in places, we serve including armor and weapons, she has allowed for me to gift each of you with a single weapon you can use in your defense." She reached in her bag and pulled out one of the swords holding it out in front of her. "These are holy swords that will burn with holy fire if you need them in battle." She activated the sword in her mind, and it burst with bright golden flames lighting up an area over thirty feet around her even in the diminishing glow of the evening. "Everyone will get one but be forewarned any hand that draws one of these swords against ShadowDancer will be burned. They cannot be used against us."

Samuel was mad at himself for getting angry with her. They were both still new at leading under the guiding hand of ShadowDancer. He would apologize to her later. He really liked Terriala and wondered if that was not part of the reason they kept arguing over little things. Maybe they both were hiding their feelings behind the outbursts of frustration. Samuel did not know how to approach the high priestess with personal questions like that, but maybe he could find a way when they were sitting together as friends. He really did hope she felt the same way, or he would be making a fool of himself.

Most of the gathering filed up and each accepted a sword. There was a group that came up separate insisting they do not use swords but asking if they could have the holy blessing on their weapons of choice. Terriala was glad to comply most used a staff of some kind and a few used finely crafted whips as their weapon of choice. There was an even smaller group who did not use weapons at all and she blessed their hand wraps with the holy weapon blessing. They all tested their weapons and made sure they knew how to bring the fire to life including the hand wraps making their hands burn with golden fire.

They selected the first week after the last of the harvesters returned to be their week of celebration. The only instructions they had were simple find activities that were fun and would promote everyone getting to know each other better. These events and programs were to include feasting, games, small group activities and large group activities. This would be their first harvest celebration, so things were not expected to go perfectly, but everyone was expected to have fun and laugh at their mistakes.

*   *   *   *

*

Bonny and Eric had named their twins after different grandparents. They were going to call their daughter Elizabeth after her mom, but Grandma Elizabeth insisted they honor Eric's mom instead and name their son after her dad. Their daughter received the name Roxanne Marland and their son Franklin Marland. After they had the children Bes, Bonny's mother Elizabeth, moved in with them so she could spend as much time as possible with her grandchildren.

Bonny and Eric both secretly tested their children regularly to see if any special abilities showed up. So far both children had been raised and schooled as normal children their ages. Both were in the upper end of their classes and liked school and time with other children. Neither had so far demonstrated any special talents for having parents with magical powers. While twenty-one years had passed on Ethar, their two children on earth were turning thirteen today. It was a Saturday, so they had all day to celebrate and have friends over.

"She was born at eleven fifteen and he was born at eleven thirty-five." Bonny was saying, "So we can have them each blow out the candles on their own cake as the right times."

"You know thirteen is one of the ages marked as a changing point in the path to adulthood. It is the age of responsibility in many societies." Eric cautioned, "If they are going to have a blossoming of power so to speak this is one of the ages when it could happen. We have told them and taught them and showed them some of what we can do. They are as prepared as we can get them. What if something happens in front of all the other children?"

"I know you like the idea of magical dates and ages for things to happen but look at the natural development of the biology we know. Things just don't happen on a schedule. You do not start puberty at exactly X number of days of life. Biology and the human mind both work independent of exact dates or time frames. At best we can say normally this happens between these ages" Bonny shook her head, "The rest is just social rules and superstitions."

"I think we have seen enough to know that some superstitions might be based on a real source of information, although you are right even those tend to be distorted over time."

They walked back into the other room where the children were all gathered around a table with their friends and grandma was entertaining. "Are you guys already to sing, have cake and ice cream?" Bonny asked excitedly.

"Yeah!" all the children responded. Each of the children had six of their friends over. Both cakes were set on the table. They lit the candles on the cake for Roxanne first. And everyone sang. At exactly eleven fifteen she blew them out. Eric saw thirteen different color flames light in a circle one at a time over Roxanne's head and looked around. The kids did not notice, but he could tell that Bonny saw them also and looked back at him. They both new what was happening and reserved any action unless there was an outward appearance others could see.

The cake was cut and small pieces were handed out before the second cake was lit. Everyone sang again for Franklin. As he blew out his candles the same thirteen flames lit in a circle over his head.

Eric captured the moment, everything around them stopped and he and Bonny were in the moment. "Those are the flames of the thirteen power sources we innately draw upon as ancients of Ethar. Not all of the ancients have access to all thirteen and these do not include other intelligent power sources like the barriers. Just because they now have the power does not mean they will automatically know what they can do. We will have to teach them control." Eric blurted out.

"Will we have to pull them out of public school?" Bonny asked.

"Not if they can keep it under control, but only you and I can tell if they use it while at school, which means one of us will have to be on earth at any given time or they will have to go with us."

"Do you think we can wait until the party is over before we talk to them, or is there a risk of something happening before the party is over?"

Eric thought a moment, "There is a risk, but I think we can handle anything that might happen. If not there is a risk from now on as long as our children are on earth."

It was Bonny's turn to think for a moment, "Alright, let's get back to the party and let this play out and start teaching the kids as soon as the rest are gone."

Eric let go of the moment and the party continued as if nothing happened. The circles of flames dancing over their kids heads unseen by anyone else. Games and activities last about another hour and the rest of the children went home.

"Children," Bonny called for their attention, "We need to sit down and have our first young adult conversation, parents and children."

"We already know about sex, mom. The kids at school have been talking about it for years now." Franklin did his best impression of a responsible adult.

Both Bonny and Eric laughed, then Eric added, "We can talk about that later, right now the five of us need to talk about something else very important that has just happened. We need to discuss responsible behavior with your new abilities and how we will start teaching you."

Grandma Bes looked at Eric and Bonny like they were trying to pull some kind of shenanigans. "You are not going to drag your kids into your mysterious games, now are you?"

"Mom, we have showed you we can do things and told you when they were born that they may at some point start having some of those abilities. Now is no time to start questioning it, because it has started, and we cannot stop it from coming." Bonny spoke firm, yet with compassion.

"Really, it is happening now?" Roxanne was bouncing with excitement. "Can we try something?"

"I think we should talk first, then we can step into an alternate world to test what you can do." Eric instructed. "This is something that you will have to absolutely never use when we are not around until you are older and have learned how to control what you can do. It may be hard to not use it by accident, but if you use it we will know and you will have to stop going to public schools."

"How can we do it by accident?" Franklin asked, Bonny looked at Eric.

"The first time I used any power, I was reading something and wanted a cup of coffee. I did not fix one, but the cup appeared, and I was sipping the coffee before I realized it was there. There was also an apple that appeared and a book I needed that I didn't even know existed till I looked for it." Eric reached out to an empty space on the table and a coffee cup appeared as he picked it up. "See?"

Roxanne responded, "So we can have things happen just because we wanted even if we are not deliberately doing something, it can just happen? We have to control what we want when we are not home?"

Bonny took a deep breath, "That would be what you dad is saying."

Eric quickly instructed, "Both of you hold out your hands and

picture your favorite fruit, apple or banana, something in your hand."
Franklin suddenly had a plum and Roxanne had a Nectarine. "See it is
simple to start doing things, the hard part will be not activating your
abilities every time you want something or wish for something. There
are things that are more complicated, but the simple things like this will
be hard to hide. Worse than changing your lunch to something you want,
what if you get mad at someone? Your anger can make bad things happen
too. You cannot go back in time and undo something after you do it
either."

"We like going to school and having friends. If one of us makes
a mistake will that mean both of us have to stop?" Franklin asked,
"Roxanne has better control then I do, she should not get in trouble if I
mess up."

"We will make a deal with you both. You do your absolute best to
keep your minds sharp and not mess up and we will evaluate any accident
that happens. You both will have to learn to have complete control over
your anger though." Eric looked at Bonny.

"We will see how that works out." Bonny was a little more
reserved, concerned about consequences if anything got out about
what they could do. Bonny pulled Eric to the side. "Does Chareece,
ShadowDancer, know she has a half brother and sister?"

"We have talked about it, but I think it was more surreal to her. She
has never met them and until now they were normal earth children who
would never know about her world. Perhaps one of these trips we should

introduce them."

"We should talk with her mother about it first." Irritation was evident in Bonny's face, "There are somethings my acceptance of does not mean I have been completely alright with. I like her and that helps, but I am sure there may be some feelings she will want to deal with before our children meet and find out they are related."

Eric was a little surprised, "I am sorry, I didn't know there was a problem."

"You wouldn't." Bonny took a quick breath, "and there isn't. Just saying she should know before we go introducing the children."

*   *   *   *

*

As the Avatar of ShadowDancer raced across the landscape headed to the southern kingdoms of the middle continent she toyed with memories of the future. Lyamy only wanted glimpses nothing substantial, she was just curious right now. She followed a thread of time forwards a short distance in her mind and and grabbed a moment of memory. She repeated the process until she had a concept of measurement. She measured off five minutes and it worked, she tried ten minutes and that worked also. She could control the time frame when she took a glimpse of what was ahead. She took a glimpse of five minutes ahead and then deliberately took a different path from what she saw. The future was not written in stone and at the very least you could change some events based on what you saw. She contemplated this on her way to Ehrbron but brought her focus back to her mission.

She was instructed to Find Mathew, save his mother Janice and unite his father Micheal back with the family. She was to help them get a new start. Lyamy knew where the boy lived and all the details of her assignment. It seemed like it would be a rather simple task.

It was pretty clear to her when she had entered area claimed by the southern kingdoms. There were military patrols everywhere and she noted a clear division between classes of people in their society. Peasants seemed to have nothing and do all the work. There was the military that seemed to be a little better off than the peasants, but also seemed to lack in general compassion for the people they protected. Then there were various tiers of upper class, from merchants, to military leaders, to social and political people that seemed to have control over money and people. She could see some of it evidenced by the interactions she could observe, and some because of what she had learned from the people back in Jenyin Sanctuary that moved there from other parts of the world.

She was still moving in her altered time faster than others could see. They may catch a glimpse of a disturbance, but when they looked nothing would be there. She was not noticed when she slipped through the gates of the capitol city of Erhbron. The city was built on a large extended peninsula with walls protecting it from any outside assault. It seemed like a very defensible and controlled access. The walls, the gates, docks, ports and streets were all heavily patrol at least at first glance. She dropped her appearance as avatar before entering the city, then pulled up her hood and slowed to normal time and speed a few blocks from the gates.

The military patrols were continuously evident on the main streets, but she quickly noticed they seemed to ignore side streets and alleys. Once she noticed a patrol take interest in activity in an alley where a fight evidently broke out. They were equally abusive to all parties involved and when they walked away the combatants, they broke up could have killed each other as long as they did it quietly. She also noted that those in the alley seemed to show more fear and respect to an individual in a black robe who entered after the patrol left.

Lyamy turned off the main street down a side street that would lead to Mathew's home. She turned right at the next corner; the Crowsblood Tavern would be twelve blocks to the left. She was a day early, but her first priority was to make sure Mathew was alright.

*   *   *   *

*

The ship heaved as they headed back to Ehrbron. Micheal thought about his wife and son, they were supposed to be taken care of since he volunteered as a soldier in the military. They were worried about his return and so it would seem they had good reason. The easy conquest turned into a complete defeat and they were sent away naked with only the food that was on the ships. The ancient ShadowDancer after a week came and provided them simple linen robes at the request of the enemy who orchestrated their defeat, to spare them some dignity. It seemed strange to attack and make an enemy and then have them care about your dignity after sending you home defeated. Nobody in Ehrbron would have been that gracious to any enemy.

He knew now it had been a mistake to join the military, but it was the only way he could see to keep his wife and son in a home and fed. Now he would return with the shame and possibly not even get paid for the time they had put in. This after the previous defeat they had faced marching against ShadowKeep would make a mockery of the military might of Ehrbron. If they did not get paid because of the embarrassment of the situation, he was also out the three months looking for ways to make payment on rent and his family would wind up in the streets or worse, debtors labor houses.

The mercenary ships had abandoned them before they started back, and two other ships abandoned the return to Ehrbron. He was glad he had not gotten caught on any of those ships, he had to get back to his family. Micheal turned his thoughts to what he had to be thankful for. He was raised as a peasant and his parents always taught them that if they look at what they could be thankful for, they would be much happier than those they served. He had his life and health. He was headed back to his family. He had hope of being able to find a way to make things better again. If they had to serve in debtor houses, they would have work for a couple years and be put back out with enough money to survive a couple months while they looked for work afterward. It may take a couple years, but they would get a new start. If the military kept him, he would still be able to visit his family in the debtor workhouses and maybe help pay off the debt more quickly.

Word came back they were approaching Ehrbron. They would probably land port the next day. The crew and men all felt a mix of relief and anxiety. It was home, but what that means would not be known until things started happening after they departed ship.

*   *   *   *

*

King Tagmerian was not sleeping well. He kept having nightmares of this cat woman that had really scarred his chest in a dream months ago. Unrest was increasing forcing him to spread his military forces out within the kingdom to police the land. Adversaries in the southern kingdoms were losing respect for the military might of Ehrbron and stopping their protection payments. His ships had not returned yet, but rumors had reached him that his armies were defeated on the savage continent.

Yesterday, the patrol that had been sent to claim salvage rights in the valley that had been destroyed by the undead army in the last war. Only the captain of the unit still lived, and he laid the bodies of his unit and their separated heads at the entrance of the castle delivering a message from the 'avatar of Shadow Dancer, an Ancient' that they were denied any rights of salvage in the land and would be accountable for the murders of the innocent. He repeated the words from the avatar stating he, King Tagmerian was 'writing his own fall'.

The kingdom was losing income sources. He hoped the rumors he heard were wrong and the shipment of armor and treasure would arrive tomorrow. Because of the rumors he called off the hero's welcome until he got confirmation of a victory. His own spies were reporting back that 'the crow' whoever that was, seems to be taking control of the capitol city and may have more power over events then the king.

The Royal Treasury was not lacking and could sustain their expenses with no income for year, but until now it had been steadily growing. He had wanted to keep that growth happening. He needed to act against one of the kingdoms that stopped paying protection money, that would force the rest back in line. Maybe if he came down harder with patrols in the city it would turn people back away from this crow fellow. He had to eliminate that internal threat, but how reliable were his spies when they are reporting this lord of the criminal world was more powerful than the king? How reliable were his military patrols when they report minimal crime on the streets, while his spies report a flourishing criminal empire?

King Tagmerian was on edge and paranoid, looking over his shoulders and in ever shadow for trouble. In his mind he complained, humans are the only race on this world without an ancient to give them guidance, I need a power to call upon for help. A shiver went down his spine at the thought of one of Ethars Ancients actually answering him. The human race stranded on a world that rejected them was on their own to fend for their own future without the help that all the other races receive and so far, they have not done bad for themselves. It was hard enough to find anyone that would help an outcast individual, who would care about an outcast race.

*   *   *   *

*

Mathew was up early. He was anxious because tomorrow was the day the Ancient had promised help would be here. He fixed himself a full breakfast and admitted to himself when he was done, he felt much better after a few days of eating right and getting enough sleep. He still slipped down the streets and checked out the alley to confirm the men that kidnapped his mom were still frequenting the house where he was sure they were holding her. She had been right, there really was nothing he could do on his own that would be remotely safe to free his mother. He was thirteen and old enough to do adult work, but still to small and inexperienced to face off the older adult men if he got caught.

They kept his mom down that back alley and took turns hanging out at the Crowsblood Tavern. None of them seemed to have jobs, unless guarding his mom was their job. They did not have families of their own, because it was just the same men that came and went, and they seemed to sleep there too. Among the people the King was not popular, they were looking for work and he was buying things for the kingdom from other countries, but to Mathew that was not as bad as what these evil men were doing taking his mom so they could use her to steal money from his family.

Mathew had just gotten back and was taking food out to eat a mid-day meal when a knock came from the door. He figured it was probably

64

their landlord coming to collect rent or threaten to kick them out, so he slipped into one of the cabinets to hide. The landlord would come in call for his mom, look around, see if he could find something to steal and then leave.

*　　　　*　　　　*　　　　*

*

Janice had lost track of how long she had been held captive. She had to admit she was not being treated badly by her captors. They fed her sparingly, but she got to eat three times a day. They let her use the bathroom any time she asked with some semi privacy. They even removed the bonds on her hands twice a day and made her do exercise to keep her healthy.

"They say your man's ship is coming in tomorrow. I really do hope this all works out for you to go home safely." Her captors seemed to be taking a liking to her, although she chose not to remember their names even though she had heard them a few times.

"It is not like Micheal will have any choice. This is a terrible thing you are doing. We are not rich, and we have no claim to the kings treasure when my husband returns, we can only hope what he gets form the military will pay our rent and feed us. At best you are taking that away from us."

"When the military pulls in big loot for the King everyone involved gets a share." He paused until she looked him in the eyes, "I was in the military once and I know. We will not take everything from you, only a share of that bonus loot."

"You know your friends are not as generous as you. I have heard them talk of how much easier this would be if they just slit my throat and ambushed him when he came to pay the ransom."

He smiled a knowing smile, "They are just thugs, I am in the employ of the organization. Things are not what they appear, and those guys will have to play by our rules. The people have been oppressed too long, but we need funds to make the changes happen. I truly am sorry your family may suffer for a time until we can deliver everyone from the oppression."

"You think you are a cunning part of a heroes call and your collaborators are being deceived, but in reality, how do you know you are not the one being deceived. Since when does a true champion of good collaborate with evil to achieve their goals, or do you really think the end justifies the means?" She gave him a hard look, "Your boss either way, is paying people to commit kidnapping and extortion, are those acts of good or evil?"

A momentary look of doubt crossed his forehead, "I was recruited from within the military, the military has taken over and changed the hierarchy of the organization. Change can not be completed instantly. I trust the work of my commander."

"This is a commander who serves the king or against the king and his vows?" she asked feigning innocence.

"I must be going now." he turned and departed the room.

Time was running to an end of events. As long as Mathew made it to safety, she could only hope for intervention of some kind to work in their favor. All she could do was wait.

*   *   *   *

*

Lyamy found the building where Mathew lived. She went to the owner's door and knocked. When he opened the door, she paid for a year rent on Mathew's home with a gold coin and demanded a receipt. The owner was thrilled to comply and accept the money, although he kept trying to look under her hood to see who she was. From there she headed up the stairs and knocked on the door of the apartment. There was no answer, so she touched the door and used her magic to turn the lock. As she walked in she shifted to her avatar form. "Mathew?" She could sense where he was. "You are expecting me to be here tomorrow. I have been sent by ShadowDancer."

A couple pans crashed in the cabinet as he climbed out. "Forgive me he said, I thought you were someone else." He looked at her and continued, "You look like she sent you, but you are smaller then I expected you to be."

Lyamy laughed, "Do not let size deceive you. Now that I am here, I need to go get your father, I'll be back in a moment." Lyamy altered time and to Mathew vanished. She knew where the ship was and slipped up behind Micheal. She placed a hand on his shoulder bringing him into her altered time.

"Micheal, I am here for you. Your son and wife need you."
Everyone around them appeared frozen in time. She pulled leather armor
and weapons out of her hidden pocket for him. "Put these on."

He looked at her with uncertainty. "Who are you?"

"I am the Avatar of ShadowDancer." She stated simply, "Your son
sent a request to the Ancients to help save his mom and bring his family
back together, so I have been sent to help."

Confused still but sensing an urgency he quickly got dressed. If
his son called for help and his wife needed saving, he needed to be there.
Besides she was giving him clothing and weapons, this was the best thing
anyone had done for him since they left Ehrbron to start with. "If my son
needs me lead the way."

She grabbed his hand, "I will take you."

A moment later he was standing in front of Mathew and time was
normal again. "Mathew!" He grabbed his son in a big embrace.

"Mathew, put these on." Lyamy pulled out leather armor and
weapons for the young man also.

"He is only thirteen." his father started to protest.

"I have carried a sword since I was eight." Lyamy dropped back
out of her avatar form and pulled her hood back.

Micheal stepped back his hand touching the hilt of the sword at his
side. "You are from the land we tried to invade."

"I am from the colony you attacked." She smiled, "No harm was
done, and you are not really an enemy are you?"

He deliberately pulled his hand away from the hilt of his sword. Experience told him he did not have a chance if she was part of what happened at the colony. "I am not. Where is Janice?" His concern for his wife was greater than any other feelings he currently may be experiencing.

"They have her in a building, a first-floor apartment in an alley." Mathew quickly offered. "I tracked them down after they kidnapped mom and have been monitoring them every day. There are five men who go in and out of the building where they keep her." He rolled out his pictures of the lay out on the table. "I have evaluated every access, but I could not go in alone. From their conversations they are all experienced in fighting and have all received some form of training."

"Your son is very resourceful." Lyamy pulled her hood back up. "We need to head there now. We need to intercept before they learn the ship returned with no treasure." She turned and headed to the door. The other two followed.

Lyamy headed to the alley. Mathew was whispering directions as they went. She knew the way, but he had gone through a lot of effort tracking down his mother's kidnappers, so she let him have his moment. When they reached the alley, it was empty.

"Alright, quiet now, no speaking and watch for anyone entering the alley behind us." She reached out and knew there were only three men in the house. They were in the front room and his mother was in the back room. Mathew had told them there were five men. She pointed and whispered, "There are only three men inside with Janice. I am going to put them to sleep." She did the ritual casting for the benefit of those with her and produced a cloud of gas, then pushed it in through the cracks around the window to the room the men were in. Reaching in with her mind she amplified the effectiveness of the gas and made sure they each fell asleep. She opened the door.

"We'll go get mom." Mathew stated as the mastermind of his mother's rescue.

Lyamy nodded her approval, "Untie her and wait till I get there. I am going to check the others and make sure our escape is clear."

Mathew and Micheal slipped down the short hall and opened the bedroom door. "Mom!" Mathew rushed in and his father followed.

The two others were halfway down the alley now approaching the apartment and Lyamy waited in the hall for them to open the door. She activated her cloak so they would not see her when they walked in. As soon as the door was closed behind them, she put them to sleep also. One of these two was prior Ehrbron military. She chose him. Observing how he fell as he went to sleep, she looked for a place where a cut might appear to have naturally occurred. Taking three droplets of blood, she used the old magic to make a temporary bond. She could use him to spy on those he mixed with.

Stepping away from these two she went into the kitchen dining area and smiled when she saw one of them had a minor cut from their glass breaking when they fell asleep. This one she made a full bond with so she could use them to spy or make them do things she wanted them to do. None of them would know what she had done when they woke up. She probed their minds enough to know their contact in the Crowsblood Tavern and their code phrases with appropriate gestures.

Quickly she moved back to the bedroom with the others. "Did you kill them?" Mathew asked.

"No, they are just errand boys. You cannot hold every soldier accountable for the actions of the whole army." She glanced at Micheal who quickly bit back whatever he was going to say.

"But they took my mom." Mathew looked a little angry and a little confused.

"Because they were ordered to do so, but they did not hurt her right? These men will all be in trouble with whoever sent them after your mom now. That is who is responsible for what happened and that is where I need to make things happen." She paused when she caught a glimpse ahead in time and turned to Micheal, "You are being called a deserter because you disappeared from the ship. They are sending enforcers to bring you back or kill you as an example."

"Sounds like the military. My family will not be safe either and this would pretty well mean they are not going to pay me for the time served." He was obviously stressed. "You will come with me to Kelleeshia and on to the Northern continent if you wish. First, we need to go back to your apartment, your rent is paid for so the landlord will not hassle you."

Janice held out her hand, "I am Janice, may I ask who you are?"

Mathew started to answer, "She's the ..." His mom put a hand on his shoulder, and he went silent.

"I am Lyamy, Avatar of ShadowDancer, Ancient to any who ask for her help, as Mathew has done." Lyamy took her hand in the manner that she had learned from other humans, they shook once and released. "Now let's get out before they start waking up."

"More came in?" Mathew asked as he stepped out behind Layamy and saw the other two collapsed just inside the door out.

"They are also asleep; they did not even see me when they stepped in." They all slipped out the door and closed it behind them. Lyamy took a pace that was quick for her small group of companions, but not so fast they could not keep up.

"You paid our rent?" Micheal asked. "How can we repay you?"

"If I need your help someday, I may ask, but you need not worry. I serve ShadowDancer and she has found favor with your son."

They approached the apartment and as they turned up the stairs Janice asked. "Isn't this the first place they will look?"

"Actually no. They seem to already know you were kidnapped and intend on ambushing him in the street near the Crowsblood Tavern." Lyamy stated. "I will go into the apartment first though just in case."

They reached the top of the stairs, and Mathew spoke out, "Wait! Someone has been in the apartment."

"How can you tell?" His mom asked first.

He pointed to a small wad of pitch on the floor up against the door. "I pressed that on the door and the stop when we left. It falls off if the door gets opened. If the rent has been paid, I doubt it was the landlord."

"That is brilliant." His dad stated proudly.

Lyamy indicated for everyone to take a step or two back. Someone was behind the door and someone else was to the side. Her fingers dances and she gave the air a push with both hands and the door swung open with force. A man's voice was cursing as he was thrown to the floor.

"Get in here boy!" A woman started around from the side of the door, her hand reaching out to grab something and froze when she saw the entire group. A string of profanity started from her lips as she backed away, "The boys has lived here alone for a month, we were only going to offer him a new home." Her voice had gone to an over dramatized pleading.

The fire in her eyes glowed under her hood as Lyamy stepped forward. "You were offered money and he fit the bill for what the slave traders will pay for?"

The man gave her reasonable distance as he worked his way back up from the floor and the woman began genuinely crying. "We are sorry. We have never done anything like this before. I swear."

"We have two children of our own and the collector was going to take one of them but offered us a bargain. We could find another they could sell, then our children would be safe for another year." The man offered. "We thought a boy with no parents might actually have a better opportunity." she trailed off as she saw through the justification she had built in her own mind.

Lyamy's claws came out and she touched them to the woman's cheek. "I should give you the mark of shame. You have earned it with your actions, both of you. Desperation is breeding evil in this corrupt city. I sense it is not too late for you though, so I will withhold my hand." Her claws retracted and she touched the woman temple. "Your fate now lies with us." Lyamy summoned their two children to the room.

"We will be accused of treachery." the man exclaimed looking at his children. "They were being held until we returned with payment or a suitable substitute."

"If you prefer to stay in Ehrbron and deal with the consequences of your decisions and status, I will not make you come with us. If you want a new start in a new part of the world where you can keep your family and get work to support them, you can come with us." Lyamy let her lack of patience show in her voice, "It is your choice, but you will not touch this child, and you would step out of my protection if you chose to stay."

"We will accept your protection!" The woman exclaimed quickly, "Anything you offer cannot be worse than what we have here already."

The man opened his mouth as if to say something, looked at his wife and children, "She is right. If you can get us out of this and into a better place, we should be thanking you not arguing the matter. This has been my home for generations, but what is here now was never what my ancestors wanted to happen."

Lyamy turned to Mathew, "I have a few things I need to take care of first before we go. Feed everyone that is here and stay inside." She used the mutual bond technique she had recently learned, "Let me know if you need me and I will be back here in a moment."

"We have things back at our place." the man started.

Lyamy turned her eyes filled with fire, "It is not safe and if you go without me you go without my protection. Discussion of this matter is done. If you are staying share your names and make friends quickly." she looked away from the humans, "Pterdin, would you do me a favor and guard these people and protect Mathew?"

"As you wish, milady." The golden dragon appeared in the room and sat down patiently at the door as Lyamy slipped out.

She stepped into the throne room from the window. King Tagmerian sat half dozing on his throne and did not see her come in. The guards were all out of the room, she could only guess they stepped out so he could take a private nap. "You have asked for help." she whispered in his ear.

"Yes, yes, but Ancients don't care about humans." he grumbled still asleep and rolled his head away from her.

"If they did not care, I would not have been sent."

He opened his eyes and looked at her. "Are you here to torment me further?" He obviously thought he was still asleep. He rent open his garments, "These scars you gave me in my dreams are still there when I am awake. The flag you tore still hangs out there in my sight every day, lest I should anger you by taking it down. And here you are you returned anyway." He looked out the window and back at her. "I do not wish to write my own fall, but I have none to guide me to anything else."

"You rule with a cold hard hand. Your people suffer and you invest in wars against the innocent." Lyamy stated simply. "You asked for guidance and I was sent. If you do not want me here I will leave you to your fate."

"You mock me most certainly, who are you and what Ancient could possibly be sending me help?"

"I am Lyamy, Avatar of ShadowDancer. She says no man asks for guidance in private where no ears can here without having at least some hope of being able to do good." Lyamy shrug, "She seems to think you may not be all evil. She also is not the only Ancient that looks after the welfare of humans."

"You are an avatar; did you not tell me I was writing my own fall? Are you here to help me avoid that or to help me fall?"

"Is it better for the people of Ehrbron who are innocent to Help you stand or help you fall? If I give you guidance it will be for the good of your people. It was my choice that your soldiers and sailors lived when they attacked out sanctuary."

"We have survived because we were hard and cold, feared by our enemies. That is what we have had to do in order to survive. How can we change that without falling victim to our enemies who live by the same rule?"

"You think you are stronger, making enemies of those who would have been glad to trade with you? Do you think you are stronger oppressing your people, so they hate you? Being foolish may help you for a time against those around you who are just as foolish, but as you earn more hate from inside and out, you are writing your own fall." Lyamy paused. "I can rip your throat out with a single claw and earn the fear of your men, but at the first sign that another might kill me would they stand for me or let harm come my way? If instead I do good for their families and give them hope and reason to care, earning their love and good will, being a real hero for the people, when trouble comes, they will lay down their lives to protect me."

"I fear it may be too late for me to change the course of these events." King Tagmerian sighed. "How can I possibly start making things better?"

"You can start by giving. Your soldiers did not fail you, you failed them sending them against an enemy you knew nothing about. Pay them and give them their bonuses for trying. Hire your own citizens to make your swords and armor, it will give them jobs to feed their families. Give your people a means to pay off their debts and earn their way. As they prosper, you will get more taxes. Help your people produce enough that they can sell goods to others outside your kingdom. You can keep a hard line to any who would do harm to your people but look to others for friendlier arrangements."

"Do you suggest I send someone back to your lands to make a friendly arrangement? They will turn us away as enemies after what has happened."

"You do not know until you try." Lyamy began writing on a piece of parchment, "You will give these names I am writing a full forgiveness of all debts and pardon for anything they have done to this date."

"Who are these people?"

"Innocent people who got caught up in the wrong places because of the pressures of desperation in your city."

"Will I remember this dream also when I wake up?"

"This is not a dream." Once he signed the papers, she put in front of him, she made five copies, leave two with him. "I will return and if you have heeded enough of my advice while I was gone you will get help accordingly."

King Tagermain looked out his window and one of the five tears in the banner was mended. "Guards!" he called. "I have a few messages I need delivered. I also want no less than six of my personal guard with me at all times."

*   *   *   *

*

She had her cloak drawn about her as she entered the Crowsblood Tavern. Lyamy knew all the proper responses for each challenge she was given and was allowed to pass. Her physical size was unimpressive, yet not so small as to draw unwanted attention. There was one attempt to steal from her and she appeared to not notice as the thief pulled away from her quickly hold the hand, he burned attempting to relieve her of some coin.

She gave minimal attention to the characters that filled the place.

She was here for one purpose. She was here to find the crow and find out who they were and what their intent was with their organization that had become quite powerful. She already had two sets of eyes in the organization from the thugs that had taken Mathew's mother, but she wanted eyes closer to the top. "The Crow" would not be foolish enough to be caught in a place like this. If the army came looking for him this is one of the first places that would go, but clues could be found here that might lead to the next tier of the organization.

She sat at the bar and dropped five silver pieces on the counter, stabbed a dagger in the counter and pointed to the keg of ale in front of her without saying a word. She moved three coins forwards one under each of three fingers then pushed the other two behind them. She was about halfway finished with the ale when she saw the peg on the wall in the mirror open and close twice. Silently she stood up and headed to the back of the Bar, but instead of going to the bathroom facility she turned where there appeared to be no door and pushed the spot on the wall, then slid it sideways, walked through and closed the door behind her. The room appeared empty, although she could tell with her enhanced abilities exactly where her observer was. She made a point of not looking or appearing to know.

"Sit." the voice echoed deliberately deceiving the ear as to the direction it came from.

Lyamy sat in the chair in the middle of the room, "The night is young."

"Who are you and for what purpose have you requested audience?"

"I am "The Cat" I have appropriated the ransom your five fools lost." she hissed.

"You take me for a fool? They lost and came back with nothing."

She placed twenty gold coins on the table in front of her. "There was someone who valued them at twenty gold for the lot. If you do not want it, I will keep it for my trouble."

The man behind the screen she was not supposed to know was any different from the rest of the wall in the dark shifted uneasy. "Tell me how you accomplished finding someone who would pay the ransom."

She stood up and turned towards the way she had come in, picking up the coins she had placed on the table. "You had a job to be done. If you seek to know the secrets of my trade, I shall simply take my business elsewhere."

"Wait." Lyamy knew he would not risk her getting away and then having to answer to his bosses why he let someone who accomplished his job walk away without getting the ransom money. He continued, "I was not seeking your secrets, I was trying to find a way to validate your story."

Lyamy deliberately edged her voice with anger, "So now you care by what means you receive your results? If it was an assassination, would you care if it was done with a sanctioned weapon?" She threw a dagger into the floor through the screen next to her interrogator's feet. "If I was coming in here to bring you harm, you would already be dead. Do you want the ransom or perhaps you would prefer I serve it to your boss in

80

your hollowed skull?"

Her interrogator fumbled out from behind the screen into the room, which is what she wanted. "I accept your service. You are good, better than I am used to seeing come into this place." He stammered slightly over his words.

"We are not supposed to see each other. This is to protect our identities." She hissed. Lyamy quickly grabbed his chin and locked eyes. In his shaken state his mind was easy to dominate. Lyamy liked being able to make the bond without taking blood. He was hers until she chose to release him. She placed the twenty gold pieces in his hand. "You will not remember my face or what I looked like. "The Cat" delivered the ransom collected."

"Yes master" he bowed slightly to her.

"Charles, you will behave in a manner that lets no one but the two of us know this bond exists. You will tell no one and you will address me in the same manner you would have before. Is that understood."

"Yes." he seemed to hesitate, then asked, "How can I serve you and The Crow?"

"You will serve The Crow as you have been doing and do nothing that would give any clue that anything has changed. You will protect my identity and arrangement, so nobody knows I am anything more then another rogue that is good at doing jobs." Lyamy reached out and checked again to make sure there were no other ear listening, "You do not report directly to "The Crow", tell me everything about who you report to." She touched his mind and pulled more information than he knew to share. She recovered her dagger from the floor and slipped back out of the Crowsblood Tavern unnoticed.

Lyamy realized tracking down The Crow would take more time than she wanted Mathew and his family staying in town. She turned into an empty alley and came back out both ends one of her headed to the home of Mathew and his family, the other to find the contact to whom Charles reported.

*   *   *   *

*

Freyie saw Lyamy move suddenly forward, and her eyes open farther than normal. "What is wrong Lyamy?"

"Nothing, I guess. I did not know I could do what I just did, but the part of me that is on the journey forgot that I was here and split into two. I am in three places now."

"I can feel it," Freyie nodded, "as I am sure the rest of our den does. You keep growing in the powers of the Ancients. Some of our own den members are uncertain how they should accept this. You are and will always be my Lyamy, but can you tell me if you are becoming Ancient to the Shadowkyn?"

Lyamy gave Freyie a hug, "I do not know what I am becoming. ShadowDancer told me she would not create another Ancient by accident, but she has also told me I am using powers that many of the Ancients do not know. I can also sense when other Ancients are near and who they are.

82

She also told me that as her avatar I can do almost anything she can do."

"How do you know you can sense other Ancients? Have you met another?" Freyie was excitedly listening sharing in Lyamy's experiences through her words.

"I have, he is an Ancient of Ethar, but he is not of our world. He is a dark-skinned human who is the high lord of ShadowKeep. Something like a king, but the leadership is not passed on to family, it is passed on to the next lord who the people respect if something happens to the previous high lord. He is the Ancient of war. He seems very nice, not like he promotes war, although I know he honors those who are valiant. There is conflict inside him."

"It was not that long ago we were both competing, fighting for dominance and ready to kill each other to gain position and power in our clan. I am so glad that even before you had an inkling of the power you have now, you at risk of everything for yourself delivered us from that dark time for our people."

"You make me sound like a hero. I have only ever done what was needed and right to the best of what I knew. There is still darkness in me as with all our kind. We are born with a deep savage hunger, some stronger than others, but the hunger is there. We can control it, but we like the taste of blood and power." Lyamy looked into the distance. "As ruthless and viscous as our past is and or driving instincts, I don't think we ever did anything as terrible as some of these humans do to each other."

Freyie looked confused. "They do things more terrible then killing each other for power and position?"

"We still act like the animals we evolved from, but they use the suffering of children to control the actions of parents. They do not share the basic necessities of life with all of their clan even though they have more then they need. They let their own starve and suffer if it does not feed their lust for money and power. Our ways came from survival, they are just cruel. Letting children starve because their parents do not have money, because they were not assigned to any jobs and cannot find work to get paid."

"So is money evil?" Freyie was not clear on what was upsetting Lyamy.

"No, it provides a means of establishing fair exchange of goods and services." Lyamy brought her attention back to where she was with Freyie. "It is those who love money and use people for their love of money that are evil."

Freyie pulled out a gold coin. "How can someone love this? It is a tool like a knife or a cooking pan."

"In the world out there, enough of those coins can buy people, time, soldiers, weapons, and armor. It can buy control and social sway. Money then becomes a key to power, then some forget that it is the power money gives them and are corrupted and lust after the money for the sake of having the money."

Freyie shuddered, "I do not know if I want to know this world out there. I have dreamed of traveling with you, but now I am not so sure."

"Let's take the children out for a swim." Lyamy stood up with a smile. She was glad her den, her family lived in the protection of Jenyin's Sanctuary.

*   *   *   *

*

Corvuset may not have been one of the more powerful of the Ancients, but he had his ways. He knew when the "new Ancients" started to appear. They were allowed to act directly in the affairs of the people of Ethar, which in his opinion made the agreement they were all but forced to sign null and void. If they could act directly in the affairs of the people of Ethar, so could he.

The kingdoms in the south of the middle continent were a perfect place for him to start. They were human kingdoms, and they had no Ancients of their own. He penetrated them through their underground criminal organizations. They were his type of people anyway, willing to do almost anything for personal gain. He had penetrated all of the kingdoms to different degrees, secretly pulling the swap of more of the people to follow his organizations.

Ehrbron was the ripest plum, the people suffering from economic distress, no jobs and unhappy with the king and military. The military are disheartened since their action against ShadowKeep was a failure and now returning from what should have been an easy conquest on another continent defeated made it easier to penetrate the ranks of the existing military. It would appear as if the people were freeing themselves from the tyrannical rule of the oppressive kings. He may even unknowingly get help from some of the Ancients that are trying to be nice to all the game pieces.

He was known by his followers as The Crow, a name he could hide behind. With the recent events in Ehrbron he was using his top henchman's secret headquarters to advance his situation. He had control of his top men; their minds were easy to manipulate. He was plotting the large scheme of the overthrow of Ehrbron from the inside. He found it irritating that petty individual issues were being brought to him instead of just being handled.

The most recent issue he ignored for the most part was the escape of someone being held for ransom. He told them to discipline those that lost their prisoner and go after anyone who helped with the escape. Then he ordered them to not bother him with these management functions, make decisions and take care of them.

He was caught by surprise when the king paid all the soldiers that worked for him and even gave them a bonus for staying committed after recent events. Then there were rumors he was making plans to do things to help rebuild the city. He may have to step up his direct involvement and remove this king himself. This would be an obvious violation as far as the council of Ancients was concerned, but there was no reason to honor an agreement that did not apply to all Ancients. His agents on the inside had not worked their way up high enough yet to be a direct threat to the king.

There were enough events slipping away from his control to arouse suspicion that someone else may be at work in Ehrbron. There was a certain amount of faltering expected as a matter of normal course, so there was still no justification for investigation. It was enough for Corvuset to put up alarms and protective precautions in case another Ancient were to seek him out or someone with powerful agents sent anything against him. He smiled an evil smile; he liked the title "The Crow".

*   *   *   *

*

Saphrine and Talmorg were between doing things when Eric dropped in and invited them to visit them and have dinner on Earth. They had only been to earth once before and that was to attend their wedding. They had to disguise themselves with normal clothing from the land where Eric and Bonny lived. It had been a very strange experience. Eric assured them that this time they would not have to leave their house, just enjoy a good time away from their responsibilities and return without losing any time in their world.

The house had changed from the last time they were there. It had been over twenty years now, maybe they just remember things a little different.

"Come in and have a seat." Bonny gestured to their couch. She poured them each an elegant glass of wine along with one for her and Eric.

"Welcome to earth again." Eric said lifting his glass and taking a sip.

"Roxanne, Franklin, please come meet our guests." Bonny called over her shoulder.

"Yes, Mommy." the two children came rushing out.

"Saphrine, Talmorg, these are our children. They were born the year we came back from our first visit to Ethar. I know time moves differently between worlds, so it may seem a little weird. They just turned thirteen." Bony turned to the children, "Roxanne, Franklin, this is the king and queen of the elves we helped on the other world that daddy and mommy visited."

Saphrine steadied her breath as she set down her glass of wine. She knew this should not upset her, but somehow, she never imagined Chareece having a brother and sister. Both children smiled excitedly bowing and curtseying as graciously as they could speaking at the same time. "It is an honor to meet you." Saphrine could not help smiling

"It is our pleasure." Talmorg responded, "Very nice children." He added looking back to Bonny and Eric. Talmorg anticipated where this might be leading. "I am certain that Chareece would love to meet her sister and brother, even if they are on or from a different world." He placed a calming hand on Saphrines.

"As Bonny just said, they just turned thirteen and to the minute their power awakened." Eric paused, "This is not normal on earth, so we were hoping to bring them to Ethar to visit and meet their sister. We did not want to disrespect you as parents of Chareece, you have raised her and Saphrine is her mom in every sense. Bonny pointed out we should not bring them together without your knowledge and permission. This is a unique situation and I hope it does not make you too uncomfortable."

Saphrine wrestled her emotions under control. She remembered suddenly her time with Eric as if it were yesterday and pushed it back into perspective. "They should know each other." She looked Bonny in the eyes and the two of them seemed to exchange more then what was said. "I appreciate your consideration Bonny. Thank you." She turned to Eric. "You may want to talk to Chareece before they meet so it is not a surprise to her when she meets them."

The matter was settled, and they all relaxed conversation ranging to more casual subjects. Talmorg and Saphrine got to know Roxanne and Franklin a little and told them a little about Ethar from their point of view. They took Eric's suggestion and stayed as guests getting some sleep before they went back. Eric returned them to a moment after they had left Ethar.

*   *   *   *

*

When Lyamy stepped back into the apartment, the two families were distinctly separated, one on one side of the room and the other on the opposite side. As she stepped in Pterdin nodded and vanished. The parents obviously did not trust each other. The children appeared to be stuck with their parents' decisions. "Alright, everyone up. Gather everything you want to keep; this is the last time we will be in this apartment." She looked at the other family, "Tell me your names."

The woman stepped forward. "I am Bernice, and this is Martin. Our children are Scott and Kara."

"When we are done here, we will go to your place so you can collect what you can carry on a long journey to take with you." Lyamy touched Bernice on the temple and got a location and image of the inside of their home. "It will not be your home again for a long while and if you do ever come back here, you will probably have a different home."

Janice walked up holding Mathew's hand with Micheal in tow. "We have everything we need from here. We really do not have equipment for traveling."

"Whatever is missing, will be taken care of, do not worry." Lyamy stated. Suddenly they were all in a different home. Lyamy pointed at the door and three deadbolt locks appeared holding the door closed. "Quickly and quietly. Next port is out of town, then I need to stop using such powerful magic for a while so they cannot use it to locate us."

Three times Bernice and Martin packed more than they could carry. Finally, even though it was more than they could carry Lyamy found it acceptably culled down and Took one of their backpacks and attached an unseen pocket to the inside so that it would open when the backpack was opened and allow them to carry their belongings that way. An instant later they found themselves on the road away from Erhbron facing north. "We will travel to ShadowKeep first."

"Aren't they our enemy?" Scott asked, tugging on his mom's sleeve.

"I don't think so, or we would not be going there." she looked at Lyamy and shrugged.

90

"They are not your enemy." Lyamy stated simply as she started leading them up the road marking her pace so the younger ones could keep up. "ShadowKeep does not choose to be anyone's enemy and even those who have lost to them are treated with the opportunity to be friends. ShadowKeep is a sanctuary, a place where nothing you did before you go there counts against you."

"Why did we send armies to attack a place like that." Scott asked innocently.

"We can talk about this later." Bernice whispered trying to avoid the discussion.

"He seems smart, we can talk about it openly, unless you have something you want to hide." Lyamy said with a slight edge in the tone of her voice.

"Oh, no, just didn't want him bothering you with silly questions." Bernice stated, "It was the King who chose war, not the people."

"Before you say too much, before I was Avatar, I started changing the ways of my society where I was raised. So, I know that the ways of a society can be changed by individuals and the blame cannot all be laid only at the feet of the leadership." Lyamy glanced over her shoulder and kept walking, "I also know that your King desperately wants to make things better for the survival of the kingdom. He chose wars he thought that you would win in hopes of boosting the support of the people. He has no offspring, so wealth is for the kingdom, not for his own personal use."

"Then why doesn't he just fix things, use the treasury to build the kingdom and feed his people? His is King right?" Martin bellowed.

"Sure, he is King," Lyamy stated, "and that gives him some power, but he listens to advisers that supposedly tell him what will be best for this or that in the kingdom. They say things like if you feed the people today, they will expect you to do it every day and the kingdom will run out of money. Or they say if you give to the people and not make them work for it they will despise you because they will be depending on you."

"There is some truth to advise like that." Michael stated, "I think if the money the kingdom spent on buying things like armor was spent buying it from our own smith or good from our own merchants, we would all have jobs and not need handouts."

"But they make better swords." Martin Mocked.

"Then send our smiths for training." Michael answered. "Or better yet, use the army for defense instead of attempting to to conquer more and invest in what our people can be good at. My blacksmith mentor was a master at crafting brass instruments."

"We have accepted our place and worked as hard as we could to find our way to a better life for our children." Janice offered in; her voice weakened with a sense surrendering to circumstance. "I am glad you came and have hope we can do better now, but even looking back I do not see where we could have done anything to change the course of the kingdom."

"There are things we can only see if we are looking for them." Lyamy stated, "If life was hard in the city, why did you not move to outer lands of the kingdom. Did any of you suggest training the local smiths to the king, perhaps by anonymous letters? I do not know what you could have done, but moving forward, always look for what you can do. If it will make life better for those around you, share a loaf of bread." Lyamy stopped and sniffed the air.

Michael the only one with military experience, placed his hand on his sword. "What is wrong?"

"There are horses coming up behind us, from the sound and smell I would say soldiers. We do not know if they are after you, any of you." Lyamy looked to the side of the road, "We can take cover behind those bushes over there and continue after they pass."

The group followed her instructions, and she did what she could to conceal any obvious trail they left. She ducked down and the others started hearing the sound or the horses approaching. The markings indicated that it was a mercenary unit, not Ehrbron Military. The horsemen did not even slow down and the broken bits of conversation that they could catch had no meaning.

"They were on the ship I when I came back." Michael stated.

"So, they could be looking for you or hired to look for either family." Lyamy stood and went back to the road indicating for everyone to follow.

*   *   *   *

*

Slipping down another back alley Lyamy made her way to meet with the next tier in the organization of The Crow. Meet may be a rather obtuse way of wording the situation. She was in fact not actually going to come face to face. She could feel his presence through the walls and new he was in charge of half the operations inside the city. She probed his mind and found that one piece of information she was looking for.

She slipped back out of the alley unseen. She was traveling invisible now making it easier to be undetected. Her next and final stop she hoped was a warehouse on the docks. Nobody could see her and while that made it easy to be undetected it also meant she had to be more careful to avoid collisions. The streets were busy and after losing time ducking and dodging through the hustle on the streets, she chose the roof tops to finish her journey, at least as much as was possible.

It was after the third roof she learned to stay near the ridge or structural parts of the rooftops. She would find a way to pay for the repair of the roof where her foot went through later. She skirted running into someone repairing another roof. She was certain that the other two people she avoided encountering on a roof here or there were thieves sneaking about. Lyamy had to drop from the roof level before reaching the docks. There was a gap between the housing and the docks.

Lyamy paused at the trellis above the docks. There was no intended access to the dock from the housing section of town. It was about a thirty-foot drop, an easy jump for a Shadowkyn, Lyamy would have no problem there. She identified the warehouse she was looking for and planned the shortest route to the back of the building. Something was tingling her senses and it was emanating from the warehouse that she was targeting.

She jumped down on the deck below. She could hear the water breaking on the wall beneath the deck.

As Lyamy made her way through the maze of dock buildings the sensation got stronger. It felt like one of the Ancients might be in that building, only if possible weaker than her. It was her intent to walk in the front door as an agent. She knew all the secret codes and passwords to gain access and talk to the big boss of Ehrbron who worked directly for The Crow. Her intent at this point was not to overthrow the organization, but to learn the intent and purpose of its leaders. It was their town and if she could find a way to get either or both sides of the arrangements to work together in a way that helped the people even if it worked out to the greed of the leaders she would. She had no intention of changing the way their culture worked that would be up to them.

Lyamy approached the door with her hood up. She made all the appropriate motions as she approached. The coded knock was simple and not unique except for the deliberate hard knocks in the sequence. The door opened and she stepped in neither looking left nor right. She could feel who was around her but followed the process to the letter. She would let the boss know who she was and why she was there when she arrived. Lyamy was even willing to pay whatever homage or respect was required to keep this a peaceful meeting.

The farther she got through the rituals the more it felt like this Ancient or Avatar of another Ancient may be the boss she was going to meet. As she stepped into the meeting room it was dimly lit, but she could clearly see the man sitting at the head of the table. He gestured her to sit at the other end. He was the boss; she could tell from his thoughts that were there without effort to perceive them. The other presence was in the room, circling behind her. She gave them her trust; she had never been given reason to doubt the intentions of an Ancient. After the correct greeting and exchange of encrypted phrases she spoke plainly. "You probably already know I am not just another agent. I have come to you to see if I can help you and your boss with more profitable arrangements for both you and the people of Ehrbron."

"What could you possibly do that my boss cannot." the man's thought gave away that the Ancient or avatar behind her was his boss when he said the word. It was "The Crow" and he was immediately behind her. Before she could respond she realized her danger and felt the black shadow blade biting its way into her right shoulder. She called her presence back from her third split, but not before feeling the blade slice completely through her exiting her lower left side. The pain was worse than the death of her construct when she sacrificed herself for the good of the clan. It was not an ordinary blade it sliced through her without pause or hesitation she felt it split her heart in two and her body start to slide and fall apart before she was removed from the room by her will.

*   *   *   *

*

The conversation had trailed to more pleasant subjects as they walked. There had been no further incidences since the horseback mercenaries passed. To Lyamy the two families even seemed to be making a bond of friendship. They even asked her about her home.

"Are you really a cat?" Kara asked, "Can I see your tail?"

Lyamy dropped her hood and showed the excited youngsters her ears and tail, "But I do need to keep them covered so people don't get weird when they see me."

"That would be so fun!" Scott said pretending he was moving his imaginary tail around.

Suddenly for no apparent reason Lyamy collapsed to the ground on one knee with a scream of pain and then whispered "ShadowDancer!" She felt the scar forming in her skin. She would bear the mark of her death in her skin, no deeper damage. That blade of shadow had the power of her blades of flame. The sensations of feeling her body severed through hung in her mind and her eyes were held open wide. Lyamy forced herself to breath and pulled herself back to where she was and who was with her.

ShadowDancer appeared rage filling her eyes, "You are my protected Avatar! He had no right. Corvuset will pay the price for this blunder. Are you alright Lyamy?"

"I think so." Lyamy forced herself to stand. "I should have been more careful, but I thought I could trust Ancients and their avatars. I knew he was behind me and I intended no harm."

"I can remove this scar." ShadowDancer gently caressed her shoulder in her hand.

"No, this will serve to remind me to keep my guard up always."

Lyamy pushed the residual sensations of death away.

"Then step apart from yourself again and we will return to Corvuset together. He is one of the weaker Ancients, he is not an avatar." Lyamy and ShadowDancer both stepped out of themselves and together the duplicates vanished. "I will travel with you for a short distance. There is a point in time we can and should not change, not long ahead."

"I have seen it." Lyamy said.

"Pterdin will be there. Drakalon taught you to see the threads of time and you have learned to use them. You received that being linked to me." ShadowDancer paused, "I am glad you know the art, but you are right, I need to be more careful when I share with others."

The others followed in silence and awe as they started moving again. Having previously been separated from even discussion of the Ancients and now to have the escort of not just an avatar, but an ancient also.

*   *   *   *

*

Lyamy was home alone for a change, practicing her forms and getting a good workout while she could undisturbed when the blow came. She dropped her sword, collapsing to her knees screaming as the pain ripped through her body. She collapsed and rolled onto her back, forcing herself to breath. Lyamy was thankful nobody else was home to witness what just happened, it would be enough to have to explain the scar. She closed her eyes and explored the sensation of dying pulled short as she pulled her separated form back to the one still on the road from Ehrbron. The first time she was in control of her construct, this time it was a split of herself and caught her by surprise. She decided she did not want to have this happen again, but she needed to find a way not to feel the pain if it did.

She picked up her sword and slipped it back in her scabbard. Sat down and began to meditate on the threads that bound her copies together. Examining them at each level of magic she had learned to control. This may take time, but she would learn to control what her copies shared. If she was successful, she would not only stop the others form experiencing the pain but be able to prevent the scarring from being shared or passing to her reunited form.

*   *   *   *

*

Corvuset appeared and gasped at the absence of his victim almost as quickly as he was celebrating his conquest over another Ancient, although he did not know who this one was. She was gone, yet her blood still stained the chair and table. He was not filled with her power, but she could not have lived through the swipe of his blade and a construct would not have had so much power as he felt in her presence. She was more powerful than he was, he could feel it. She did not have her guard up her thoughts even shared with him the goodness of her intent, which would not help his cause as she had thought. His cause was to bring the city down and rebuild it to follow him. If she helped the people before the government was overthrown, then the people would not rally behind his orchestrated overthrow.

"She is gone. She should be dead, but I have a feeling she has escaped death also." Corvuset rasped. "Not even an Ancient can live with their heart split open, surely she was pulled away by another and has not escaped death."

"Surely." his boss of Ehrbron nervously agreed.

"Even if she is working with another, at the very least this will delay their interference in our work." Corvuset seemed to relax slightly and put his blade away. "Step up our schedule. We need to bring chaos before some other interfering force decides they have an interest in this region ripe for the picking."

"Perhaps she was an agent from ShadowKeep?"

"She was not. She was a cat from the savage continent. She was brought here by another, but ShadowKeep has no interest in the affairs here or they would have stepped in years ago." Corvuset paced the floor and stopped. "She must have been associated with others weak in power or they would have protected her sending her in here. They will not dare try anything, but we will increase our security anyway." Suddenly he shivered at the presence of power that was in the room out of nowhere.

"You dare act against my protected?" ShadowDancer's words struck him hard enough to make his footing uncertain. He felt her disarm all his security as with a single thought.

He tried to exert his anger as he turned, "Who are you to come into my house and reprove me for defending my interests?" He saw Lyamy standing next to the powerful ancient and knew even without her protector he was no match for her.

Lyamy stepped towards him. "I came here to see if we had room to negotiate. My interest in this kingdom was nominal at best. If we had no common ground, I would have left this festering pit to its own means. My interests are in other places, but you have now given me reason to take real interest in events here."

He may have made a mistake with this one he considered in his mind. "You came in here with your intent clear and what you intended would have interfered with my work. I did nothing more than defend my interests."

Lyamy reached out exerting her will, eyes locked on his, forcing his will into submission. He had a lot of power, but a weak will making it surprisingly easier than she had expected. She reached out and nicked his arm with a claw and drank in five drops of his blood. She bound him with three different sources of power, including the old magic. "I bind you to me. You are no longer your own. You are mine. I own you." The piece of his being that she took within her was a bigger rush of power and exhilaration than any other she had taken to this point. A sweet savor of a drug that too easily could be addicting. She brought the passion quickly under control. She had worked to long and hard to allow the nectar to draw her from the cause of doing what was good and right.

"Yes, Master." He tried but could not stop himself from responding with the words he uttered. This was new, something he had never seen before. She now had power over him.

"You have met my avatar." ShadowDancer said stepping up. "Fortunate for you she chose to keep you as a pet. I was just going to make you suffer and leave you broken and dead or worse than dead." ShadowDancer smiled and looked at Lyamy, "She finds ways of solving things without killing, one of the things I love about her."

Corvuset looked at ShadowDancer, anger he could not unleash filled his eyes. "We are Ancients and you have allowed a lesser race to take control of an Ancient. The council will not forgive this."

"Where to begin?" ShadowDancer feigned being at a loss. "Will the council forgive you for taking direct involvement in the affairs of Ethar after signing the accord not to? Oh, and maybe you see me as a lesser race then you also, since I was born of an elf? Now what would my Father say to that?" She glared back at Corvuset.

"Perhaps I am hasty in my judgment." Corvuset started getting a grasp on his situation as his anger gave way to realization. "If other Ancients are allowed to act directly in the affairs of this world, then the accord that was signed is null and void."

"Sit." Lyamy instructed Corvuset as she sat down herself. "As I understand things, only Ancients that were not here when the accord was signed have acted directly in the affairs of this world, making you the first to violate the agreement. Even those who did not sign have stopped any direct involvement." She looked at ShadowDancer.

102

"That is correct. See my Avatar knows my mind and she is allowed to act independently. She could claim status as an Ancient, but even as an Ancient would still be my avatar and still be just as free to do as she chooses. What you call her does not matter, she is more powerful than you and has subjugated you. You could have found yourself with a harder master."

Lyamy leaned forward and gestured towards the city underworld boss at the other end of the table. "You have a boss in every one of the southern kingdoms here. You can make them your avatars. They can act on your behalf, but you can no longer act directly. It really is just a small step back. You will not overthrow the kingdoms, but you will keep them in balance."

"Uniting them would make things more stable for the people. Wasn't that your end goal also?"   Corvuset shrugged, "I was just going to unit them under my rule."

"They need to choose their own path. We can influence those choices and protect individuals or groups, but overall, we need to let them make their choices. If their choices result in unification whether by war or peaceful means it is theirs." She turned to ShadowDancer, "I am starting to understand that some things I do as me a part of this world and somethings I need to treat a little more detached."

"So, you are going to just leave me to do as I please for the most part now anyway?" Corvuset was perplexed.

"You will feel compelled to do her will. You cannot hurt her. She can see everything you do including your very thoughts. There is really no reason she cannot leave you and at any time she chooses she can take control of your actions too." ShadowDancer laughed, "I think that about sums it up."

"If the king does good, this city and kingdom will prosper. If it prospers your avatars will prosper also. Either way your influence will be strong."

Corvuset looked at ShadowDancer, "So did you pull her back and save her life?"

ShadowDancer shook her head and smile. "No, she did that all by herself."

"How?" Corvuset looked back at Lyamy.

"If you do not know, it is probably better I don't tell you."

ShadowDancer took Lyamy by the hand and the next instance they were in a room with Melina and a couple other of ShadowDancer's messengers. "Are you sure you do not want that scar removed. You are doing at least as well as I have done at learning to handle having power."

"It will provide me a warning next time I consider trusting someone I don't know behind my back Ancient or not." Lyamy looked at the scar for the first time. "It seems to be a clean line, not at all ugly. It may cause my den some worry, but it should also provide them some comfort that I cannot be so easily killed."

"You have a wisdom of your own. You know I would have simply killed him if you had not stepped up and taken such command over him."

"I know." Lyamy answered. "I saw a weak will wielding power. I see the Ancients now as everyone else only with power. Some take responsibility for what they can do, others become victims of their power letting it control them. Perhaps coming from a hard beginning has helped me see the responsibility."

"Would you consider me one of the corrupt or responsible ones? You know I never had it hard like you did. When I was not an Ancient, I was a princess." ShadowDancer looked out the windows that showed her people in different parts of the world. "People from every part of every society make choices good and corrupt, to blame their upbringing or environment is just an excuse, the decisions were theirs. The corruption was theirs. What you have shown me though is sometimes, some can be turned back from that corruption."

"If his will had been strong, I would not have been able to pull him back from what he had done." Lyamy saw the sanctuary through one of the windows and smiled, "So maybe we just have the willful good and the willful evil and the rest that just follow the influences around them."

*   *   *   *

*

They walked down the road several miles before ShadowDancer Vanished. The only one who knew she was really still there was Lyamy.

"So, you can talk to an Ancient any time you want?" Scott asked.

"I can, and so can you. It does not always mean they are in a place to hear you or that they will answer. Sometimes they are busy, but normally they will eventually get to hearing your request."

"But humans do not have Ancients like other races." Martin stated.

"That changed some twenty years ago. The ruler of ShadowKeep is a human and an Ancient, as is ShadowDancer's father and his wife. So, there are three Ancients that are human."

"You mean our king tried to go to war against an Ancient?" Micheal seemed surprised.

"He did not know and was misguided." Lyamy tensed ever so slightly, but enough for Micheal to place his hand on his sword again. It was the mercenaries that has passed them earlier. There was an ambush waiting for them around the next curve. She signaled to Micheal what was ahead as she spoke. "You have to be willing to forgive people for their mistakes or you will spend your whole life being mad and getting nowhere." She indicated how many on either side of the road. "You have to know when to pull people together and stand in their defense and when to let others take care of the rest."

Micheal nodded his understanding. As they rounded the corner, he put his arms out slowing everyone down except Lyamy who walked straight into the ambush drawing her swords as the soldiers started leaping out of the brush. Lyamy moved with Shadowkyn speed disarming them as they appeared. Micheal guarded the group and whispered "Backup."

Lyamy had most of their attention and weapons. "Surrender before it is too late she hissed.." She leaped over the two closing the gap in front of her and slammed their heads together while she was still in the air causing them to hit the ground before she landed facing the group that was closing in on her. "I missed one." She yelled for Micheal to hear.

The four around her had rope out. It was obviously their intention to try bringing them back alive. Lyamy kicked up her speed, grabbing the ropes out of their hands tied their feet together and looked back to see the last one had engaged Micheal and they were going toe to toe in combat. The group of four fell to the ground entangled and twisted all of their feet bound and pulling against each other as they struggled to get back up. Two daggers flew from Lyamy's belt. The soldier fighting Micheal dropped her sword as the blade sank in the back of her wrist and dropped to her knees as the other sank in her calf behind her shin guard.

Micheal pulled the rope from her belt and bound her as Lyamy turned back to the others sprawled pulling against each other on the ground. "Surrender and be spared." she pulled her flaming blades out and the mercenaries realizing their position stopped struggling. "How much were you offered for returning who from this party?"

"We had three contracts." One of those now sitting not struggling against the ropes stated. "One Contract for the soldier and his family delivered to the Crowsblood Tavern at two gold per head. One contract to return the soldier to the military authorities for six gold. The last contract from the slave traders a gold each all to be sold as slaves to pay their debt."

"So, sixteen gold for the lot of them and no mention of me?" Lyamy toyed with her blades in the air, "Should I be offended?"

"No bounty for you we would have let you go. Perhaps minus a few weapons."

"Are you willing to make a new deal? You are soldiers of fortune for sale to the highest bidder, are you not?"

"That is how we make our living. What kind of deal are you going to offer?"

"Well to start with what would be the consequences of you bringing in someone who had the king's pardon for all their offenses. Let alone eight of such persons?"

"We were not told anyone was under a king's pardon." a touch of fear actually showed on the soldier's face.

"I really do not know the consequences, but they do have the king's pardon, all of them. I will pay you for safe escort to ShadowKeep. Two gold each now in advance for your services and another three gold each upon their safe arrival."

It was apparent the speaker was the leader. "We will agree to that. First we cannot bring anyone in who has a king's pardon and second you are offering us more for their safe passage then the contracted bounties."

"Untie yourselves and gather your gear." Lyamy went over to the soldier on the ground by Micheal and grabbed her daggers cleaning them and putting them away. "Let me see your hand."

"It will never have the strength to hold a sword again." She held her hand where Lyamy could look at it.

Taking the seriously injured hand between her own Lyamy wove the blue threads of magic and in seconds the hand was mended and whole again. "Now your leg. You cannot defend these people if you are lame." The leg was healed as quickly.

The woman was obviously impressed stepping back as she picked up her sword and slipped it back in the scabbard at her belt. "You do not need us. You have the powers of the Ancients."

Lyamy found it curious a human who openly spoke of the Ancients but let that go. "Are you declining the offer?" She was simply asking not intending it to be a hidden threat, so she was a little surprised at the woman's reaction.

With a touch of alarm in her voice, "Brandon is my captain, I would never renege on any agreement he has made. I did not mean to imply we would do anything less that what he has agreed to." She glanced at the leader of the group for a moment and looked away as if hoping not to be noticed.

The ways of these people were not familiar to her, Lyamy was not trying to cause trouble for the soldier who she had just recruited. "I am Lyamy, what is your name soldier?"

"Sargent Amie Poole at your service." she snapped to a posture of attention.

"I am not familiar with your protocols and customs. Can I count on you to provide me with instruction in this area as I need it?"

Amie looked over to Brandon who gave a nod. "Yes, I can provide this service for you."

The two she had knocked out were back on their feet and their captain Brandon was explaining events to them. Lyamy handed Brandon a twenty-piece gold coin. "You can split this appropriately with your soldiers. Let's form up and get moving."

"One question." Brandon spoke with slight hesitancy. "Can you assure our safety when we get to ShadowKeep. We have never been known as friends there."

"Captain, if you are not safe in ShadowKeep, then I would not have offered the bargain. Do you think I would spare you, heal your soldier simply to march you and your team into a trap. Amie was right, I am able to defend these people on my own. Your escort is more about politics and educating your people. Consider this a political mission. When you return to Ehrbron you will file a report with the king and drop a copy of that report sealed at the Crowsblood Tavern with instructions to deliver it to 'The Crow'. You will put in this report an honest sharing of what you observe."

"You know we contract our services with the king, which does not play friendly with this crow fellow. We are merchants, but we do try to stay on the lawful side of those who contract our services."

"Dropping this report off will serve the king, you will not be violating that trust. Although you may leave out the part about being defeated before we struck the bargain, nobody needs to know you lost a fight." Lyamy moved forwards with the captain in the lead. The two families were behind them and the soldiers took up positions behind and to the sides. Idle conversation was slow to start, but the journey to ShadowKeep was several days. It was the innocent questions of the children that eventually opened conversation between the mercenaries and the families, and a subtle bond started building.

*   *   *   *

*

The Crow, Corvuset sat there for several minutes saying nothing after ShadowDancer and Lyamy vanished. He looked up at his Ehrbron boss, for the first time seeing him as a potential peer instead of an inferior servant. "Things are changing everywhere. Call off the rally, we do not want to start a revolt anymore. We are going to take a new approach."

"As you wish, they did still leave you in charge. No offense intended, but are you playing a new game or are you complying with their instructions?" The boss was tentative in his questioning.

"You know how you cannot hide secrets from me? Well, I can no longer hide thought or intent form her. Secrets would be out of the question. I do not know how to do what she has done to me. We have been given liberty to continue to operate as long as we comply with the restrictions she has specified. We no longer have a bid to rule and unite the kingdoms, but we can still manipulate influences on the direction things go. We can rule the underbelly and sway anything we choose."

"So, business as usual, just no overthrow power plans." he shuffled some papers he had been looking at. "There is truth to the thought that we can make more profit off a city that is prospering then off one that is collapsing. We do have control of the legal and illegal lending facilities.”

Corvuset stood up. “And we have agents at almost all levels in the government and military. Perhaps we already have the power we wanted without the visibility. Adjust activity to encourage business with our percentage for protection. Limit slave trade to outside captives and not debtors, we can use those in debt to other ends. If we can give them a way to pay back their debts, they will owe us and we can use that influence.”

“According to the reports I just received; the king is started pushing prosperity packages. He is using money from the treasury to help rebuild business within the kingdom. It seems our rally and power push would have backfired with these new programs drawing support for the king.”

“We have enough influence we; you can decide where these funds are invested so we can reap the most profit and still let the king gain some reputation with the people.” Corvuset walked up the underground boss of Ehrbron. “You are elevated to my primary Avatar. You will assume the title ‘The Crow’. The bosses from the other kingdoms will report to you.”

“So, with all respect I am taking your job and you are taking a less hands on position?”

“That would be a correct assessment. I will still be able to deal directly with my Avatars and each boss will gain that, even though they will also answer to you.”

“Perhaps we should give a name to the organization? Maybe ‘The Order of the Crow’?”

112

"You can call it what you want. We will all meet in two weeks from today I will call you all to the location." Corvuset vanished.

*   *   *   *

*

Darvarias resided in ShadowKeep most of the time with his father Hans, HonorLord. He was half jinn and had learned much about his mother's people before he lost her in the last war. He went north and visited his jinn grandparents regularly, but as the son of Hans, the Ancient of War. He too was one of the Ancients with the fullness of the powers that put that power at the tip of his thoughts. His father did not know exactly when he started to manifest the power, although he had offered many times to assist him with learning to use such limitless power.

His father rarely used the powers of the Ancients, so Darvarias had taken to visiting Darvel in the Shadow Realms where he could practice and learn without effecting the world, he lived in. Darvel was one of the oldest Ancients and was glad to teach the young immortal everything he was willing to learn. Darvarias felt at home in the dark elf kingdom that served Darvel. Something to do with the power and the cross breading with a jinni, his skin was much like theirs, lighter than his fathers, but with the slight translucent effect of the dark elves.

Darvarias had also heard the stories that traveled around concerning ShadowDancer. As the son of the High Lord of ShadowKeep, he had met the first-born princess of the Kingdom of Talmorg many times. He liked Chareece and knew while her mother was the queen, her blood father was Eric the most powerful of all Ancients and best friend of his father. Chareece was ShadowDancer, but she maintained separate identities and most of the world did not know they were the same. Darvarias had not defined his place in the world like she had, but recently he had taken to spending time with Chareece to learn from her also.

They were both high on the walls of ShadowKeep talking with a few of the dragons who were holding human form to make it easier. Eric appeared facing them. "Hello kids." He laughed knowing they did not think of themselves as children anymore.

"Hello Father." ShadowDancer gave him a big hug. "To what do we owe the pleasure of your appearance on Ethar? Your manner gives away this is not just a random drop in."

"Ever perceptive." He smiled with a touch of pride. "Before I tell you, I am going to ask you not to get angry. You probably will have every right to since we never told you sooner."

ShadowDancer did not like the lead in. "You know I do not get angry easy. Please drop the buildup before you get me primed to be angry and just tell me what you have come to share."

"Your brother and sister on earth that you have never met born the same year as you on earth, but with the time differences, they only just turned thirteen." He paused and tried to read her expression, but there was nothing to reveal her thoughts. "They have come into their power."

"You should not have hidden me from them for so long, keeping me a secret."

114

"It was not really a secret; more it never came up. They were on earth and you on Ethar and you would probably never meet. It was a bad decision, and we apologize, but with no evidence that they were more than normal earth children, well it would have been harder on them having to deal with an alternate reality." Eric felt he deserved some anger but hoped to avoid it.

"I need a moment to digest this, twenty-one years to find out I can finally meet my sister and brother." She thought it through, she probably would have still seen very little of them and they were now half her age. "You do know they have been no more than a distant concept in the back of my mind until now."

"Should I leave you two in private?" Darvarias asked.

"No." they both answered too quickly, but for their own reasons.

"I will withhold reacting for now anyway. So why twenty-one or thirteen year later is there a change of heart?"

"Before they were mundane, just normal earth children in a world where magic is not real and for all we knew they would stay that way. They were living in a world where magic is not real and to actually believe in magic would tend to make them outcast. To the minute when they turned thirteen, they each received the fullness of power. They now have magic and need to be taught anyway. There was no longer any reason to keep Ethar a secret from them. I thought you should at least know each other and meet if you choose to."

"And?" she persisted.

"And nothing." Eric expressed with slight exasperation. "Sure, you might be able to help them learn control and whatever, but we can teach them that without bringing them here. You know we can form a universe and world to be their playground if we wanted to. You are related, and at the very least should at least meet each other once."

"Alright, father. I will not be angry or react all crazy, there is enough anger and hurt in the world. This was a big one though and you owe me now." She smiled. "I would love to meet my brother and sister. Does mom know you are bringing them here? Oh, or did you mean for me to go there?"

"I had not really given a lot of thought as to where to meet. I mean I figured here, but you have been to earth before."

"I could drag Darvarias along, he should see the world his father came from also."

"I am sure it would be alright, but Hans might want to be there the first time his son sees earth."

"Hello Eric." Hans walked up to the small gathering. "I felt you arrive and thought I would come see what was happening. And Yes, I would like to be there, but now is as good a time as any."

"I'll take us." ShadowDancer stated. And in an instant they were all in Eric's living room standing behind him before he vanished headed to Ethar.

"You can time travel?" Eric asked looking at ShadowDancer.

"Time threading is something I have manipulated before." She looked at her Father, "I was sure it was something I got from you. Drakalon warned me not to alter fixed points in time, it could cause serious problems."

Eric looked thoughtful for a moment. "I have wondered but have not tried to toy with time. It did seem a little strange to me that the time differences between earth and Ethar were not consistent."

"That was quick." Bonny stated, "Hi Jamis and Darvarias and should I call you Chareece or ShadowDancer?"

"Bonny, you can call me whatever you want." ShadowDancer changed her appearance to that of Chareece, princess of the Kingdom of Talmorg. "Probably best to call me by what form I am using in case others are around."

"Eric explained the situation I am sure. I take the blame and responsibility for the secrecy, if you need to be angry with someone, let it be me. As long as they may have been normal earth children, I felt it best for them to have no ties to anything beyond that. In retrospect I can see we probably should have told you even if we were keeping it from them."

"Bonny," Chareece interrupted stopping her monologue. "You acted like a mother protecting her children. I will not fault you for that. I will just need a little time to process relationships. You have always been more like an aunt to me, because I have my own mother. You made the choice not to hate me or my mother a long time ago. I choose not to be angry or hate anyone for what has been done and can not be changed." She smiled at Bonny with mischief in her eyes. "We can just blame Eric and tag team him right."

Bonny laughed as much as a stress release as in appreciation of Chareece's humor. "Roxanne, Franklin, come meet your sister from Ethar." she looked back to Chareece, "This is all new to them also."

Hans put a hand on Darvarias shoulder, "We should probably look appropriate for being here." Their attire changed to appear as typical clothing that Jaffro Jamis would have work before he left earth the first time. "Come with me and you can check out the home I have here. It is actually rather spartan and I really only maintain it for the benefit of Bonny and Eric." The two of them headed out the door.

Chareece eyed them leaving. She had wanted Darvarias there for support in her emotional turbulence in discovering family she should have known about. Her sense of need felt too immature to stop Darvarias from leaving with his father to explore his own roots. As the two younger half siblings rushed into the room Chareece committed their looks and the feel of their presence to memory. "I am Chareece." she stated with a slight bow of her head.

"You're a princess." Roxanne observed, "I am Roxanne, and this is Franklin."

"I can tell her my own name." He held out his hand as if to shake. "I am Franklin."

Chareece bent over enough to hug them both ignoring the offer to shake hands. "We are siblings, we should know each other as such." They returned her hug although with a little less certainty.

"We have to hide what we can do from other people, so we do not scare them here. Do you have to do that where you live?" Franklin asked looking anxiously at Chareece.

"Sometimes I do." Chareece answered, "It is mostly because I need to hide that I am both the elven princess and ShadowDancer." She shifted between the two different appearances.

"We have not learned how to do anything like that yet." Roxanne lowered her eyes.

Chareece looked at her knowingly, "I need a few moments to talk with Bonny and Eric, er," she looked slightly perplexed, "Our father and your mother."

"Alright." Roxanne groaned as she spoke and grabbed her brother dragging him back in the other room.

"Chareece?" Bonny asked inquisitively.

"They have the fullness of the power I have, maybe even more. There is a lot they need to know and as soon as possible if they are going to avoid blundering like I have." She looked between Eric and Bonny as they both looked back anticipating more. "I learned methods of sharing knowledge from the Shadowkyn and have improved on those greatly, so they do not require dominating or stealing essence from each other."

"Aren't they a bit young to have such knowledge, wont it be dangerous to let them loose on earth if they do?" Bonny was obviously concerned.

"Isn't it more dangerous letting them go out there and accidentally burn down some building or eliminate someone who made them angry because they have not learned to control what they can do? You are parents it is your decision." Chareece shrugged.

"I am interested in these methods of sharing knowledge either way." Eric stated, then looked at Bonny. "She has a very good point. Roxanne and Franklin have a much better chance of not getting into trouble if they know and understand what they have. Remember when we first had power, even though you were shielding and protecting imagine if you had done that here on earth before you had learned to control what you had. Woman discovers she has strange powers dissection at eleven."

"So, you are in favor of them sharing in a full knowledge?" Bonny had to admit to herself it would be less dangerous if they had enough knowledge to control what they did. "Alright, I'll go along with this, mostly because I cannot think of an alternative. Share with us this knowledge first though please."

Chareece opened a family bond with Bonny and Eric. "I have nothing to hide from you guys or my brother and sister. I can hide or keep things locked away of share fully with you this way." She showed them how the bond worked. "This is a voluntary bond, any of us can leave the bond if we choose to. As long as the bond is active though, we will know where the others are and have access to any knowledge, they are willing to share."

"This is a great way of sharing, although I see the methods you derived it from were rather viscous. The Shadowkyn have a very savage background, although honestly what race that naturally evolved does not" Eric observed. "They are considered basically adults at the age of thirteen. That was true of humans once also."

"We can bring Roxanne and Franklin into this." Bonny said, although she knew Eric and Chareece could now both feel her hesitation. "You are here and back in the City of Talmorg right now. Are you always in two places now?"

"Sometimes as many as nine, but yes always at least two." Chareece answered

"Eric?" Bonny looked at him, "You too? How long have you been keeping two?"

"Almost since we learned to do it. It makes it easier to take care of responsibility in two worlds." Eric smiled and hugged them both. "Let's bring the youngsters in."

"Roxanne, Franklin." Bonny called.

The two came back in and Chareece placed a hand on a shoulder on each and pulled them into the shared awareness. They drank in the knowledge that had become available to them and discovered the greater capacity of their minds then what they could do before they turned thirteen. "You know," Chareece began looking back at Bonny and Eric, "if they split, they could remain here and return with me experiencing both worlds also. It would give them a means to release without displaying power here on earth."

"We have not created a world we can observe from as you have

Chareece." Bonny noted. "We have been observing from here. Perhaps we can share world you operate from? I do not want to impose if you want to keep it private."

Chareece laughed, "I don't mind, but the rules are different there. Some of those living there are dead, like my messengers. All I have there is a few rooms and, not really a world. I had not taken the time to define anything else."

"There is no rush." Eric stated, "Shiheel has already offered us a place to stay and work from any time we what on Ethar. The ancient Gaharias has offered us to visit his place also any time we wish, and he is family too. We also have the option of opening our own places which we can do any time we want or even make a shared place to work from."

Bonny nodded, "You are right, of course. Even though I have had these powers for almost fourteen years I am still new to all this. I suppose I have not completely stepped into accepting it is real. I will take your advice Eric and do the whole two of me thing so I can be in both worlds at the same time. Perhaps that will help."

"You have a career here you feel strongly about." Eric stated. "That is your anchor to the reality here. You have accepted the magical enhancement of your medical abilities here and intellectually you know that could not exist if the rest was not also real. We also have not aged in thirteen years. At some point we are going to have to do something on earth to conceal our differences form the rest of the world."

"Let's do this." Bonny said stepping out of herself so that there were two of her standing there. "Go ahead kids, give it a try." She changed her appearance so that her clothing was appropriate for ether, on the copy of her that stepped out. Eric, Roxanne and Franklin all followed suit. They split into two groups the one staying and the one going.

"What about Hans and Darvarias?" Chareece asked, changing into ShadowDancer.

"They will return when they are ready." Eric shrugged, then added, "Besides we will all be here still to tell him what is happening."

ShadowDancer brought the group with her back to the parapets of ShadowKeep.

*   *   *   *

*

Magus Kremlern was the oldest, most prestigious, most powerful Magus in Kelleeshia. He liked power he studied magic his entire life because he liked power, but he had declined any office on the city council beyond consultant. He even pushed for the laws that forbid any Magus from having a position in political office. It was his considered opinion that a lust for power can corrupt and that gaining position in too many platforms of power could make Kelleeshia and the people of the country fall victims to someone who might succumb to such powerful corruption. He had added that anything a good Magus would want done the council would see to anyway.

He had enemies among the other Magus who would have jumped at an opportunity to merge political power with their Magus status. Magus

Kremlern was surrounded by a magical fortress of protection that was not as obvious in the gaudy facade. In the heart of his fortress, he guarded the portal to the Sahdowkyn. They were considered by Kelleeshia a potential threat being form the Savage continent and the council charged him with protecting the city from anything that might come through. He considered the threat to be greater the other way around, although the Shadowkyn would be much more capable of defending themselves then any intruder might expect.

He was concerned there were rumors of a dark Magus raising armies. There was word on the docks of pirates and merchants recruiting soldiers to get revenge for a recent defeat. He gave warning to those at Jenyin Sanctuary, and they seemed to take it in stride. They were different than other peoples. Even after mixing with others they still did not place high value in material possessions. They were not lacking though for either. They were a society that had an abundance of resources and freely distributed necessities to their people including money. It was also expected that everyone pitches in and do work of some kind to help the community. What amazed him is that everyone that lived there did. There were no people that chose to be lazy and not contribute in any significant way. The community had a bonding he had not seen anywhere else.

Kelleeshia was in contrast a wealthy city built on business and to no small extent greed. They welcomed the poor and downtrodden but did not take care of them. They were a potential resource for profit or political advantage. The city was governed under the laws of the council and this

124

was one of the greater cities of mixed influences. The council was half human and then scattered other races. Human cities on Ethar were always mixed with other races at least to some extent. Some believed it was because the other races wanted to keep tabs on what they did. Kelleeshia was the most welcoming, there was money to be made off of everyone.

Magus Kremlern ran one of the most prestigious academies for magic. Unlike others he taught more than one school of learning. Arcane was the biggest student body, but they also had schooling for divine and nature magics. He also ran a school for less known arts of magic for those with aptitudes and abilities that fell outside of the traditional magics. He did not school in necromancy although Necromancy and Divine magic were the same schooling just different application, so his students of the Divine learned some Necromancy at least enough to know how to counter it when they had to. Other than the capital cities of the other races Kelleeshia was the place to go if you wanted to learn magic. It was also the most central trading port in the world.

With the vast extent of variety and business Kelleeshia also had one of the largest standing armies in the world intended as a peace keeping force. The army never left Kelleeshia or the lands around the city they protected. Kelleeshia had patrol boats to protect the harbor, but no ships for carrying troops overseas. The Military patrolled the docks, city and surrounding areas. They served as both defense force and police force. Their locations of service were continuously rotated to avoid corruption by familiarity. The military was well paid, and you could not be a member if you had any history in corrupt venues such as piracy or mercenary.

There was corruption in the politics, but even the politicians supported an incorruptible policing force for their own protection from each other. The only thing that could threaten the balance the military imposed would be a battle between Magi. The order of the Magus governed the interactions between powerful casters in the city and anyone who violated their rules would be forbidden to reside or practice anywhere in the country. They may not be able to enforce it, but they even applied this ruling to any Ancients who should happen through. Magus Kremlern was perhaps the only one they might not be able to force to comply without a war. He had no intention of challenging the order of things, after all it was under his direction the order was in place.

"Hello, Magus Kremlern." his security jumped, but almost immediately relaxed back to alert positions when the recognized ShadowDancer as she appeared in front of the Magus where he sat.

"Hello, ShadowDancer. To what do I owe this honor." He gave a slight bow of respect to the demigoddess.

"First thank you for assisting with helping Lyamy." She handed him a book titled Kremlern Compendium 2. "Only a few are powerful enough to use this magic. I expect you to continue to use wisdom and not cause me to regret this trust."

Kremlern's eyes lit slightly. "I am bound to honor our agreement." he looked up with a whimsical smile. "I have no desire to start breaking agreements, let alone incur the wrath of a gracious goddess."

"There have been fluctuations, ripples in the background layers of magic. I have gotten glimpses of warriors from another world being brought into ours in threads of the future. The location is not consistent, but the arrival is. There is an someone who is serving as a power apex from this world pulling them across. If you hear rumors of anyone tampering with unknown power, let me know."

"Of course. What does this army look like?" Kremlern inquired.

"Their skin in widely varied in color almost as if paint was randomly thrown at them, but it is their natural color. They are a humanoid race, slightly larger and their looks are fiercer. They have larger sharp teeth, claws and were wearing the hides of beasts and enemies. They were mostly using weapons, but some wielded magic. Baratir is what the race is called or of the bear."

"Perhaps it is something one of the displaced Ancients is working on?"

"No, I am pretty sure they are summoned by someone from Kelleeshia. The arrival is a fixed event in the time streams. You remember I told you there are some things while I have the power to change them are too dangerous to change. One of the many locations they may arrive is here in Kelleeshia. They are not evil, but people will die wherever they are summoned. They are being pulled from the middle of a war and they are being summoned with the intent of causing violence."

"I will put our feelers and let you know anything I learn." Kremlern stood up. "I will also reenforce defenses here and look for methods of subduing an army without violence. Perhaps recruit the aid of the Shadowkyn. At the very least I will meet with them and let them know of the threat so they can be prepared to help if needed." He looked back at ShadowDancer, "With your permission of course. Are they also a location of direct risk?"

"They need to be aware also, but I want to wait until Lyamy is on the northern continent before she finds out. For now, you are the only one with a glimpse ahead, because I need you to find out what you can."

*   *   *   *

*

Melina stepped through the window appearing by the statue where Terriala was meditating. "Greetings Terriala."

Terriala opened her eyes her eyes coming to rest on Melina. "Sister, messenger of ShadowDancer, it is a delight to my eyes to behold you again."

"I would that I were bringing good news. I am delivering a warning from ShadowDancer. You and Samuel need to be prepared to rush to the aid of Sein Estel even as I am tasked to warn them to be prepared to come to your defense."

"We are in danger? How much of a threat?"

"I do not know what the threat is. Something is coming and she wants you prepared, although she also said she is not sure where it will happen and wants everyone prepared anyway."

"Delmar and Peltricia were not exactly happy with us when the left. They did not want to follow our rules, which the governing and organization fall under Samuel." Terriala took a deep breath, "They have always been allowed to come and go from here freely, but they also have separated themselves from me as ShadowDancer's Priestess. Perhaps we do not need a priestess at all."

"The people wanted a priestess and ShadowDancer gave them you. There is no fault of yours if those do not follow in your favor. They are already suffering in that they do not have weapons with your blessing giving them power. You stand between service to ShadowDancer and those who would turn her followers to serve something else in her name."

"Thank you, Melina. You have given me something to think on that may lift my spirits. I will let Samuel know we need to prepare for an unknown battle that might not come and in so doing be ready to stand with our people in Sein Estel. We are all followers of ShadowDancer."

Melina gave Terriala a hug. "I must continue and give Delmar and Peltricia the message also. See you again soon." Melina acknowledged to herself that ShadowDancer was exceptionally gracious to her allowing her to be a messenger to her sister. She was the only person ever sacrificed on an alter to ShadowDancer. ShadowDancer honored her but told her people never again. She was taken to serve as a messenger to give her death some purpose.

She shifted to ghost form to travel faster and headed to Sein Estel. The land was beautiful as she sped past and she did feel some regrets about having lost with her sacrifice the ability to fully appreciate all the sights and smells and sensations of life. She was too young to know what she was giving up at the time. It was however no longer a part of her to be saddened by things, that was a sensation she also no longer experienced on Ethar. She was welcome to stay in service to ShadowDancer as long as she chose, but also free to move on at any time she chooses.

Even though she could feel she was no longer alive out here traveling Ethar when she was back in the place ShadowDancer had built for her she felt alive there. She could taste and feel and smell her food. She could feel the floor and objects around her. When she was there, she could feel her emotions and she would have to ask ShadowDancer about that when she returned. When she reached Sein Estel she went straight to Delmar and Peltricia through the back wall of the town meeting hall.

"Greetings Delmar and Peltricia from ShadowDancer." she said as she appeared in the table in front of them.

They bowed their head partway I honor to her. Peltricia spoke. "We are honored to receive the messenger of ShadowDancer. I hope you bring good news for our people."

"I deliver a warning and instructions. ShadowDancer until now has only told her people they had to do one thing and that was not to sacrifice anyone on an alter for her." Delmar and Peltricia both looked nervous. Melina continued, "The warning first; There are events coming that are not yet clear, but they may threaten your people or the people of the camp at the shrine. There is trouble coming the location just is not clear. You are being instructed to prepare everyone to defend Sein Estel or the southern camp if either come into harm's way."

"Why would we rush to their defense, we left to get away from their oppressive rule?" Delmar was obviously disturbed at the idea of submitting to the authority of Samuel's camp. "Are they willing to do the same for us?"

Peltricia put a hand on his shoulder to calm him down. "Delmar, I am sure she will do her best to answer questions, do not get animated over issues before you know they are real."

"Thank you, Peltricia." Melina smiled. "Yes, Samuel and Terriala have agreed to come to your aid if attacks occur here. You are free to rule yourselves or wander free as you choose, Samuel and Terriala have made no motions or effort to take away any freedom from the followers of ShadowDancer. Samuel leads those who follow him, not all of ShadowDancer's followers. I will remind you that Terriala is the only priestess designated or chosen by ShadowDancer and you would do well not to forget that."

"Can we have a priestess in our camp, someone dedicated to the goddess that can guide us in these matters?" Peltricia was calculating her thoughts behind the innocent look. "I mean Terriala is the High Priestess, but there could be others who report back to her who could share the will of the goddess with the rest of her people."

"I will let ShadowDancer know your request." Melina smiled warmly. "Was there anything else you wish me to communicate back or that you would like to ask about?"

"Can't we just ask things of ShadowDancer ourselves? Why would we need a priestess?" Delmar did not like the idea of someone else telling them things they could or could not do.

"You can. She does her best to consider every request that she receives also. Even whims are considered." Melina laughed lightly. "However, consider; If you had a priestess before she would have been able to stop the sacrifice before I was placed on the alter. A priestess would not tell you how to live, but she would give you guidance before you made a grave error. She would also be able to place divine blessings upon your works. Everyone in Samuel's camp has a holy blade because they each have a sword that was blessed by Terriala. Perhaps if you each pay homage, a visit and respect, she will bless a weapon for each of you?"

Delmar took a deep sigh. "I did not mean to offend, and you are right. We do not have to follow Samuel to visit the High Priestess. Peltricia has shown wisdom in asking for a priestess in our midst."

"We serve the same goddess." Peltricia stated. "We should be friends and allies. I am sure if we keep asking or pushing issues, she will give us rules. We are free from rules right now, but if we get rules because we pushed for them, then we will have to follow those rules and be bound no longer free because we asked for it."

"And a priestess would not take that freedom away, but she could give you guidance if you started making any serious mistakes." Melina nodded. "I must return. We will meet again."

This time as Melina vanished she appeared back in the room with the windows where they could observe the followers of ShadowDancer around the world. "Hello Lyamy."

Lyamy turned from the window where she was watching herself marching toward ShadowKeep. "It is nice to see you in person Melina."

"You can have a few minutes if you like." ShadowDancer sat in a chair near them. "You need to let go of this persona; I am sure that holding three is starting to strain a little. It used to be difficult for me at first."

Lyamy looked between Melina and ShadowDancer. "In the Sanctuary I am sleeping right now, here I am minimizing my thought, so really the only focus I am holding is on the road to ShadowKeep. You have honored me letting me come to your personal home. I am always honored by your messenger and I think of Melina as a friend, but I will pull this copy back and not overstay my welcome." Lyamy bowed graciously to ShadowDancer, faded and was gone.

"Melina, you did well as always."

"They want a priestess in Sein Estel. I am sure that Peltricia thinks she can influence what a priestess would offer if they had their own."

"I am sure she can as long as she is not going against my will. Just as Terriala has told our followers on occasion that some of what she offers is her thoughts, not my commandments. She talks to Samuel; she does not tell him how to govern his people. Any priestess for any location will refrain from overstepping any governing body unless I specifically instruct them. They will be trained by and answer to Terriala."

"So, you are not leading your followers?" Melina had a touch of confusion in her eyes.

"No. I simply helped people that needed help. I have not searched for followers. I asked them to help others because in a world that has enough food to feed a hundred times or even a thousand times the population there is no reason for anyone to go hungry other than selfishness and greed. There is some balance though too. I cannot just give everyone everything they will become dependent and weak. There has to be some challenge and some effort required. They choose their path and if they look to me I will guide them where I can, but I cannot claim I have more wisdom then they do concerning how they govern themselves. I am twenty-one years old and there are those in the world that are ten times my age. I am not saying age equates to wisdom, but someone who has shot an arrow before has a better concept of compensating for wind and distance then someone who has never seen one."

"You still amaze me." Melina stated. "You have all this power and you have not elevated yourself above others."

*   *   *   *

*

Lyamy touched the minds of each of the mercenaries. None of them had any thought of dishonoring the contract they had made with her. She noted that most of them even liked the idea of being contracted to help instead of bounty hunting. A couple had just been mercenaries so long they did not know how to do anything else, and a job was a job. She could have the beginnings of her own personal army if she wished.

The part of the country they were now traveling through fell under the general jurisdiction of ShadowKeep, but it was undeveloped and unclaimed land. They had barely crossed the halfway point between Ehrbron and ShadowKeep and the landscape while not mountainous was a little hilly. There was light foresting mixed with fields and underbrush. The land was not populated or developed. At any point along the road a community could be built with everything they needed to survive and prosper. The only shortcoming would be the lack of any natural means of defense from any hostile military force. There were resources that could be used to construct a defensible fortification.

The sun was low on the horizon. There would be perhaps a couple more hours of sunlight. "Sargent Poole, take someone with you and meet us an hour up the road with some meat from the hunt."

"Yes Ma'am." Sargent Poole and one of the men turned off into the woods galloping off on their horses. They would move faster than the rest of the party since they were pulling two wagons, they had bought from a farmer outside Erhbron for the families to ride. They moved a little slower to keep the ride from getting too rough. Lyamy checked the wagons. The children looked miserable; their parents did not look that much better. The humans were soft and used to sleeping on bedding, not riding on wooden buckboards with the exception of Micheal who was a trained soldier.

As they slowed and came to a stop, they were in an open area surrounded by tall grain stalks. Lyamy knelt on the ground and pulled steel from the ground forming it in the shape of short swords. She handed each member of the two families a blade and suggested they harvest some of the straw to make pads to soften their ride and sleep on. The hunters showed up a few minutes later they had dropped two small herd animals, perhaps a hundred fifty pounds of meat. It would be enough to last them the remainder of the journey.

The two women of the families, Janice and Bernice were using their apron to catch thrashed grain from the stalks they were harvesting. The soldiers had cooking gear, so they were taking the grain and filling pots. They diced up a variety of tuber that had been foraged a day or so earlier and mixed it in the pot with water and meat. Lyamy had a campfire going and Captain Brandon had set up a tripod to hang the cooking pot. They prepared two pots, and everyone ate a hearty meal. While they ate several pounds of meat were soaked in seasonings and then hung on makeshift rakes over the fire. The racks were high enough not to get too hot, but to be caught in the billows of smoke from the fire. Left all night the jerky would be divided among everyone in the morning.

Lyamy instructed the children to work with the guard that were stretching and scraping the hides from the animals that were brought back. They were also puling and stripping animal guts for spare bowstrings and for cord for sewing things. Breaking the sinew down to various size threading for different purposes, including field surgery, something soldiers learned out of need. The parents did not question Lyamy's instructions, she did not know if they were afraid or in agreement with her, but survival skills are always good to learn.

"How much further do we have to go?" Micheal asked. "This is not easy on the untrained."

"At the pace we have been going," Sargent Poole offered, "it will take another twenty or thirty days. We somehow jumped a significant distance more then we have traveled already though, so I really cannot be sure."

Lyamy laughed, "I have used magic several times to shorten our journey already. We will reach the gates of ShadowKeep in two days. There were reasons I was not to completely skip this part of the journey. Some of those reasons were for me, most were for you, but all things will be revealed in their time."

"So you could have just gone poof and had us at ShadowKeep at any point along this journey?" Janice seemed a little irritated.

"And you guys would still be at each other's throats with no reason to try to get along, your children would not have learned valuable survival skills. There have been more benefits to the small amount of traveling we have done on the road. Still your anger, I am here at your son's request for help. If you can get better help elsewhere please feel free, I am not keeping you bound to me in any way."

The changing thoughts were obvious in the expressions on Janice face, from anger to shock, to frustration and then turning to tears. Lyamy really did not understand the tears. She did not see anywhere that the woman was hurt enough to force tears and could not imagine enough pain to cause such a shower of tears. "Are you hurt somewhere?" Lyamy's genuine concern only caused Janice to cry even harder. "I did not mean you harm, I do not understand how I hurt you?"

"You have done nothing wrong." Janice blubbered.

"She has just hit a stress limit." Bernice pipped in giving Janice a hug. "Crying will help relieve the stress, just give her time, she will be alright."

Lyamy nodded, not really clear on what she was nodding about. "Take care of each other. At least you understand each other." Lyamy walked back to the fire. She realized she had power, but really did not understand much of the world around her. Through the eyes of her magic, she saw the bond between Janice and Bernice growing stronger. She knew that this would make the bond between Micheal and Martin would get stronger. She stared into the flames hoping quietly that she would gain wisdom and understanding and avoid making mistakes with the power she held.

"Why does she cry when you are nice to her?" Kara sat down asking with more innocence then Lyamy was expecting.

"I don't know Kara. I think it is something human, but I don't know everything. I have no desire to hurt any of you, and pain is the only thing that I know causes tears." Lyamy answered, in her mind Kara was close to thirteen, close enough to being an adult to speak freely around.

"I don't think you did anything wrong. I think sometimes we have things that hurt on the inside more than being hurt on the outside. When mommy yells at me, that hurts more than when she spanks me. I think it is

138

something like that." Kara said in a simple matter of fact manner.

Thoughts began cascading in Lyamy's mind. She started seeing how her life had been driven in part by feelings. There was pain she felt when her people suffered. She was driven to help others because the pain she felt at seeing them hurt. Even seeing Janice cry caused her pain inside, although she would never have thought that pain could lead to tears. The avalanche of recognition gave her some relief that Janice would be alright.

Back at the sanctuary Lyamy stuffed blankets and pillows in her unseen pocket. She pulled them back out at the wagons covering the bed of straw on each and placing pillows and extra blankets so that the two families could sleep well. At the very least perhaps they would be a little bit more comfortable and a little less stressed. She left instructions with Captain Brandon to keep moving the next day and she would catch up.

Lyamy did not need to sleep, in the blink of her eyes she could get a full night's sleep. Time would stop and she would sleep and rest and return fully restored. This was a special gift that ShadowDancer had given her. These people were safe this night, the mercenaries would take shifts protecting them. Lyamy shifted into her avatar form and vanished into the night. She raced through the night to a farm that was in the middle of nowhere. There were no roads leading to or from the farm. There were only a few families that lived there, and they had a small self-sustaining community.

There were less than a hundred members of the small community, but too many to fit in the house when the avatar of ShadowDancer arrived.

"I am Lyamy avatar of ShadowDancer, your requests for help have been heard and I have been sent. I have been given knowledge of your situation." The elderly woman was laying in the bed obviously in great discomfort. Lyamy laid a hand on her shoulder and took the pain away for at least a spell.

The woman sat up. "Thank you."

"Gramma you are alright." a young lady said, perhaps twelve years of age.

"There are some things I can do for you." Lyamy held up a hand holding back questions. "There are certain events that should not be changed in the time-line. If I never came, you," she reached out and caressed the young lady's chin, "would not be able to learn any more of your grandmother's medicine. You would instead go to ShadowKeep out of necessity for training. Events will happen that are needful to occur. A series of events would happen where grandma would not be able to tend to the medical needs of members of the farm that would result in a young man. Jeff also going to ShadowKeep in six months for blacksmith training."

An older gentleman that was the leader of the community spoke up, "You would not be telling us this if you did not intend on making changes to certain events. Tell us what our part of this bargain is that we may consider the agreement."

"I will give you a list of events that you must absolutely commit to doing. It is a short list and not hard. If you do not do everything I give you,

140

time will attempt to correct itself and the correction will be much harsher than letting events just run their course without my help. Either way you will lose your isolation but only to ShadowKeep. I assure you the high lord will give you all the respect you ask." Lyamy pulled a roll of paper out of her hidden pocket and handed it to the older gentleman.

He read down the list, pausing and looking at different people in the room. "I do not like opening our doors to the outside world, but if you are correct, we have no choice anyway. I can assure you we can adhere to this list."

Lyamy pulled out another scroll. "That was not a can-do list, that was the absolute must do list. This is the can-do list to keep other events in order."

The older gentleman looked her in the eyes understanding showed on his face. "I will see to it. We will do what we can with the second list also." He tucked the two scrolls under his arm. "Please tend to the purpose that brought you here."

Lyamy turned and touch his wife again. Her color filled in and she smiled. "You are a sweet young lady."

"I do not know if this will give you a longer life, but you will live out your life healthy. ShadowDancer trusts that you will do the things that are required that will protect you from the repercussions of changing time."

"Is there anything we can do for you?" The older woman said standing now.

"All ShadowDancer ever asks of anyone is to help others. I am her avatar, so I only ask the same." Lyamy stepped up her speed, vanishing in the eyes of the people around her. She headed back racing across the forest and fields to catch up with her two protected families and their escort. This was Lyamy's fourth side trip between Ehrbron and ShadowKeep, but the first time the party would be aware. She trusted the mercenaries and Pterdin was following in the air above the party, just in case anything happens.

As she approached the party it was shortly after mid-day. Lyamy folded the threads of time and space and the party did not even notice as they stepped from where they were to a half day's travel from ShadowKeep. Unless someone was focused on something specific, they may not have even noticed any scenery change. The landscape all had the same basic features, except now if they looked up, they could see the mountains of ShadowKeep in the not-so-distant view.

*   *   *   *

*

"So, we can use our powers here?" Franklin asked excitedly.

"You must use restraint here too, young man." Drakalon said in his natural dragon form.

"Whoa, a Talking dragon!" Franklin his voice filled with awe.

"Calm down Franklin! Remember how mom and dad always told us learn what you can and think before you jump in." Roxanne said with firm authority.

142

"I know sis, but sometimes it is fun to jump in first." he rolled his eyes whispering, "Girls never just jump in and have fun. Yes, sis, I'll behave."

"You have a wise sister; you will do well to listen to what she has to say." Drakalon chortled.

"There is a lot of knowledge and experience you have acquired through the family bond, both of you. Pay attention and use what you learn." ShadowDancer instructed. "You will have plenty of fun along the way but start by learning."

"You used your power on earth." Roxanne had a tone of disapproval in her voice.

"Yes, and I made mistakes. Our father had to do some clean up and cover up to avoid problems that could have resulted." ShadowDancer made a chair and sat down where they were on the parapets. "See I made mistakes and learned from them. You can learn from my mistakes and I am sure you will make some of your own that we can learn from too."

"She is right." Eric added, "We are not born knowing and understanding everything, so we all make mistakes and do our best to learn and do better. We have the potential of making very big mistakes, so we have to be that much more careful about what we do."

The sun was coming up over the mountains and the area they were in was being bathed in the warmth of the morning glow. "We are here on Ethar, and there is not a war that has brought us here together this time." Bonny said appreciating the burnt umber rock walls that jutted up around them and circled Shadow Valley below. The view of dragons taking to the air and landing on other portions of the parapets was enthralling. "And we do not have to worry about leaving and getting home on time. Is it always like this being in two or more places at the same time?"

Eric and ShadowDancer both started to give different answers at the same time, but ShadowDancer paused deferring to Eric response first. "Not always, right now we are in two places on two different worlds with separate time flows. Sometimes time passes faster on one and sometimes faster on the other which is different than being in two places in the same time flow."

"Yes, there are difference depending on what you are doing and where you are when you are in multiple locations simultaneously, but overall, it is always like this in the sense you are totally aware of what is happening in every location and you have to focus each of your separate selves on the place they are. Right now, there is an added factor that we are with each other here and back at your house, having a different conversation with the same people." ShadowDancer shrugged. "So, there are always differences, but generally it is always the same."

"This is so much easier to learn then school was before. I think it will make school easier too." Roxanne stated as she searched the knowledge she had gained. "Your avatar had a system for teaching her people magic. We could use that as a starting point for learning what we are doing."

"It will take time to process everything you know, Roxanne.

You will sort it out to an order that you will understand and work with." ShadowDancer stated

"She was almost our age when she became your avatar." Franklin noted. "There are lot of races that consider us at our age to be adults."

Eric laughed, "Young adults mind you. Note you would still be considered under the guidance of more mature adults, at least in most of those cases."

"Your avatar is approaching ShadowKeep." Roxanne looked in the direction she was coming from as if she could see through the stone walls and mountains.

"Hans, or HonorLord and Darvarias are on their way back. They came back to the house and visited there for a while first." Bonny noted. A moment later HonorLord and Darvarias appeared back on the parapet with them.

"Bonny, I think we should let the children here visit with their sister. Perhaps you and I should go visit the City of Talmorg or exploring? Give them some time to get to know each other." The two of them vanished from the Parapet.

"Our guests are arriving." HonorLord stated as he walked up.

"We can all welcome them." ShadowDancer answered his unasked question. HonorLord lead the way in and down. Darvarias followed with ShadowDancer in the back behind the younger siblings.

*   *   *   *

*

"Stay seated." Janice told Mathew again as they turned and started up the second ramped portion of the road on the side of the mountain leading to ShadowKeep. The gates were at the top of the road. The small comfort of padding while they slept seemed to make a world of a difference. Lyamy noticed both families were much happier, easier to get along with, and less emotional with the better sleep and more comfortable ride.

Lyamy suddenly paused, looking up towards ShadowKeep. She felt the distinct presence of at least five ancients, none of which were weak like Corvuset. The dragons had a way of keeping their power hidden, although there were enough dragons living at ShadowKeep with enough power to remake worlds that was not what she felt. She could sense that there had even been more present that had already departed.

"What is wrong?" Sargent Poole asked as the trail of their small caravan caught up with Lyamy.

"Nothing." Lyamy pulled herself mentally back to the group of companions she was traveling with and pushed the power she could feel to the back of her mind. ShadowDancer was there, so it should be alright. "I have only been here once before and did not take the time to enjoy the wonder of this place."

Sargent Poole knew there was more Lyamy was not telling her. Nobody gets that look on their face if there is nothing. "You had a sense of alarm to your expression, perhaps I over read the situation, but you looked like you were reacting to something more then we can see."

146

"I was, but it is not a threat, I was just surprised." Lyamy did not want to explain more. Sargent Poole continued with the rest of her unit. Lyamy worked her way forward again to take the lead position to the caravan. They doubled back onto the final stretch to the top. Lyamy sped ahead to avoid delays and let the guards know who they were and why they were here.

"We have already been informed." The guard offered. "We have been waiting for your arrival, although were not expecting a military escort."

"I will vouch for them if need be."

"They are with you; it is not an issue." The guard held up a hand. "You have no need to explain. Our instructions were simple, we are to let you and your companions in. There is a civilian diplomat waiting inside to show you around."

The gates were open, so Lyamy stepped in to introduced herself to the diplomat.

"Greetings Lyamy. I am Preston. I have been assigned to be your guide and make you feel at home while you are here." He looked back at those cresting the climb to the gates. "The guards will assign someone to taking care of the carts and horses."

"We appreciate the hospitality." Lyamy pointed to the families as they dismounted form the carts. "Would you see to their belongings. Make sure they get to the rooms where they will be staying."

"Do you wish to go to your rooms first and freshen up before meeting in the main hall?" Preston asked anxious to please.

"I think I can take care of that without a delay." She used the alaquine power source to clean the road dirt and disarray from everyone in the area. She followed that weaving a few more spells to refresh and energize everyone. "There I think we are ready, unless we need to dress special for this occasion?"

"My instructions did state this is not a formal meeting. You can come as you are."

Lyamy introduced Preston to the rest of the party and let Captain Brandon introduce his Unit. Instead of introducing them by name he simply stated they were known as Gray Squad. With her thoughts Lyamy asked ShadowDancer if there was anything she needed to know before they got to the meeting hall. She felt a calming sensation returned with a simple answer that there was nothing to worry about. She turned to the rest of her companions. "When we reach the main meeting hall we will be in the presence of Ancients or gods and goddesses depending on how you wish to call them. Show them whatever respect you have been taught or would give accordingly. You have no need to be afraid, they wish to help not hurt us."

Her words had the opposite effect of what was intended. The families huddled close together whispering and soldiers seemed even more nervous than they already were. They moved in silence through the hallways. Pausing outside the door to the assembly hall. Preston motioned for them to wait and stepped in. A moment later they were announced, and

Preston gestured from the doorway for them to enter. They were escorted to the front of the room each stopping where they were told to behind chairs at one of the tables closest to the throne.

When they all had stopped Lyamy bowed her head slightly to the assembly of Ancients in front of them. "It is an honor to have audience with all of you."

The others scrambled to show some kind of respect and vocal ovations to those before them mixed with apologies for various indiscretions.

HonorLord held out his hands in a quieting motion. "Please relax, you are not being judged or on trial. You are here as guests and it is a matter of fortune you will have the privilege of meeting other family members today." He waved to the seats they were standing behind. "Please, sit. We will all enjoy a meal together. I am HonorLord, known by several other names, High Lord of ShadowKeep. I am pleased to see solders of the southern kingdoms with the courage to visit on less then hostile terms. You all have sanctuary here as long as you need. Anyone who comes on friendly terms is always welcome to come and go as they please." As he sat so did the rest of the Ancients and everyone else followed suit.

ShadowDancer looked around the table as they sat. "I think we can simplify introductions by going in a circle and sharing who we are. I am ShadowDancer, Ancient or goddess whichever you prefer. I am the daughter of Eric part of the new order of Ancients. About twenty-one years ago access to Ancients was open to humans when Eric, Bonny and Hans came from earth and became the beginning of the new order. This is my world I was born here, and I care about the future and the freedom and balance of choice for the people that live here." She turned to Franklin who was sitting to her left.

"I am Franklin. I am ShadowDancer's brother. I was born on earth."

"I am Roxanne. I am also Franklin's and ShadowDancer's sister born on earth to Bonny and Eric. We are new to Ethar and to having power." She gave Franklin a look like he should have shared more.

"I am Darvarias, son of HonorLord and Stralina who died in the last war. ShadowKeep is also my home. Lyamy followed and then the two families. By the time the rest of the soldiers had finished their introductions everyone was starting to relax enough that they could speak more comfortably.

There was conversation about earth. There was surprised conversation and some sense of hope that humans now had access to gods on Ethar and what that meant to their place in the world. There was admitted astonishment that ShadowKeep did not see anyone as enemies unless they acted as enemies. Rumors of the tortures performed on humans in ShadowKeep were surprisingly evil and scary.

"I always wondered why such an evil kingdom as we were led to believe existed in ShadowKeep would not come down and conquer the southern kingdoms. We knew from the last war you had the power. We were taught from children to fear and hate you." Sargent Poole stated.

"This is a sanctuary from the world around us." HonorLord said setting down the drumstick he was holding after realizing he was gesturing with his food. "We have no desire to dictate the lives of the world around us and we will live at peace to whatever extent we can with our neighbors. This may sound strange coming from the god of war or Ancient of war, but enough wars happen and will happen without encouraging them. All options are necessary in order to allow people to have the freedom to make their own choices."

"Choice and freedom are important." ShadowDancer picked up. "Moving ahead the destiny of this world will be based on the choices of the people. Look at Lyamy, yes, my avatar now, but before that she was an individual in a society who decided to make choices of her own and change the direction her people were going. As a result of her bold stand and free choice she saved her people and changed the future of a continent. My point is no individual has to settle for what they have been given. It is what is inside you that gives you the opportunity to rise to something more."

Janice put her hand on the shoulder of her son Mathew. "So, you are saying we are not bound by the fate or destiny we were born to?"

"In part." ShadowDancer leaned forward slightly as she answered. "You cannot change that you were born a human and there are some events that are anchored in time. Mostly though your life is written by the choices you make, and you can make choices that will change the course and direction of the people around you especially if you can pull them into the choices you make."

"There are times when you cannot give everyone the freedom to make their own choices though." Captain Brandon objected. "Like in the military, it is not acceptable to have a soldier say, 'I am not going to fight this battle.' or chose in the middle of a fight to support the other side."

Darvarias laughed. "Your soldiers make those decisions every second they serve with you. Without that choice they would not be loyal comrades they would be tools like your sword doing exactly what you make it do. If your soldiers were that way, they would not be free to deviate from your instructions and defend your back from something unexpected."

"That is one of the reasons that summoned armies do not fight as well as untrained farmers." HonorLord added. "They do not have the independent thought and use numbers to balance out skill."

"Those choices are restricted if we live in a society." Martin voiced his objection. "We do not have freedom to make our choices if we have laws that tell us we cannot do things." He looked down as if something in his own mind was answering his objection.

Lyamy responded turning to him. "You still have choices. You can leave the society if you object to the laws, or you can work on getting them changed. You really have a choice not to obey the laws, although you may have to deal with the consequences."

The conversation droned on dealing with social and political concepts and philosophy through dinner. When dinner was done, they were all offered and accepted a tour of ShadowKeep and Shadow Valley. Afterward they were all shown their quarters and given freedom to do as they pleased.

Lyamy met with ShadowDancer and her sister and brother in private. ShadowDancer explained that they were visiting and learning from her. "Give them the choice to stay or go on with you. We know what choice they will make. Then I need to step up the schedule so we will teleport you all to Kelleeshia."

"The mercenaries were my call to hire, I know that was not on your list of things for me to do." Lyamy smiled. "I am letting them go but would like to keep them on retainer to call upon if I choose in the future."

"Yes, you found a means not to have to kill them all and then make good use of them as a resource. I think you have earned some loyalty from them already and having a contingent you can call upon seems reason able. You, Lyamy are of this world and as a member of your society act accordingly as you see fit. You are not just my avatar. You are at liberty to plant your influences as you see fit."

"I have started hearing whispers of voices from around Ethar." Lyamy paused, "I think they are people asking for help or favors, but the voices are not clear yet. You said that one day I will be on your council, you did not mean as your avatar?"

"No, I did not." ShadowDancer did not elaborate.

"Alright then, I will take care of the matters we discuss in

Kelleeshia and we take the Next ship to the Wall City of Talmorg. More immediately, this evening I will let the families make their choice to travel to the northern continent with me."

"Go enjoy some of the evening in ShadowKeep while you can. Meet and make friends." ShadowDancer waved her to the door back to the main assembly hall and throne room of ShadowKeep.

As Lyamy left the room, she looked back over her shoulder and bumped into Narcole, the dark elf consultant to HonorLord. Initially she thought his skin was similar to her translucent elusive appearance, but closer examination she saw clearly it had a dark oily black appearance of polished black stone. He was about as yielding too when she bumped into him.

"Pardon me, Narcole."

"Lyamy, forgive me, I should not have been standing so close to the door." He smiled and she sensed his roots were as savage as her own.

"Passage to your world is here in ShadowKeep? Is your world as intriguing as you are?"

"My world is in another dimension." Narcole responded.

"I know, but I can sense the portal beneath us, and your thoughts give it away."

"Perhaps one day I can show you."

"That would be wonderful." Lyamy smiled and continued on her way.

She headed towards their quarters. Her intent was to find the two families that were accompanying her and ask them if they were going to accompany her on her full journey or remain. She found them outside the quarters. They stopped talking and said hello to her as she approached. She smiled and returned their greeting.

"I was going to ask you all a few questions, but first you all seem a little troubled, so first I will ask what troubles you?" Lyamy was genuinely concerned.

"There are so many nice things here and we really need a few things, but we have no money." Mathew piped up.

"Mathew!" Janice was embarrassed at her son's forwardness.

"Well, it is true mother."

Lyamy held a hand up to stop the conversation. "It is alright. You have been uprooted. Even though you had little, you had the resources you knew to take care of your personal needs. I have brought you here, I will give you the means to manage until we can get you the means to take care of yourselves." Lyamy gave each of the families a small bag with coins and handed each of the children a handful of coppers and silvers. "Before you go off and spend money, I need to ask you a few questions about where you are going from here."

"You are more than generous." Micheal said with amazement as he opened the small bag. Martin and Bernice also added their agreement.

"It is a small thing." She dismissed the matter of money. "I am going from here to Kelleeshia, on to The Walled City of Talmorg and then to visit with ShadowDancer's followers on the northern continent before I return to Ehrbron. I need to know if you wish to go with me and how far. If you travel further with me you come as companions, not as protected fugitives. You are safe here if you stay, but this is a great opportunity for you to see more of the world and learn a little about other people and the way they live."

The younger members filled with excitement at the prospect of adventure so much their eyes appeared to sparkle. Both women showed some apprehension putting their arms around their children protectively. Micheal spoke first. "I was a blacksmith before business went bad, perhaps I could offer services elsewhere or learn new skills that will help us provide for our future." Janice shrugged her acceptance.

Martin picked up on the opportunity Micheal hinted at. "I was a shop keeper trading in imported goods. Traveling to other lands could give me contacts that might work with me to establish new markets. The craftsmen here have many products that would have a market elsewhere. When Erhbron was prospering I could have sold hundreds of the red stone carving I saw at the market here along with other items of crafted skill."

Bernice took a deep breath and sighed. "Then we travel with you, Lyamy as far as you will have us or until we can safely return to our homes. I will insist you let us do what we can to be a contributing part of this as companions."

"Then keep in mind what is ahead as you spend or hold money. We will be taking a shortcut to Kelleeshia so only take what you can carry. They will store anything you wish to leave here until you call for it or return. After we teleport to Kelleeshia we will spend a few days there before we board a boat for the northern continent."

"Kelleeshia is the legendary city of magic." Scott whispered to Kara.

"Yes, it is." Lyamy laughed. "Most human cities shun magic, but Kelleeshia embraces it. I have been there a couple times now. It is a very big city too and a trade center for the world."

"How much time do we have before we depart?" Martin asked obviously with purpose now behind his question.

"We shall be leaving by midday tomorrow. I will see you in the morning." Lyamy turned with her Shadowkyn speed, she wanted to explore the market and Shadow Valley.

*   *   *   *

*

The Delucette academy was one of if not the least reputable schools of magic in Kelleeshia. They were not too concerned with reputation, most of their clients were children of pirates. They had very few graduates and taught on an as paid basis. "You pay us a gold we teach you one gold piece worth of magic no questions asked." They had a pact with the thieves' guild trading skills and protection. Needless to say, most people avoided the part of Kelleeshia where the academy and the guild could be found.

They had a couple ships of their own, but their docks would only accommodate the long boats nothing big enough for either of their ships to dock. They had been performing salvage operations in the northwestern portions of the cliffs of the middle continent. The ships would stay out far enough to avoid the rocks and salvaging of wrecked vessels was done by diving from the long boats they would row back and forth from the ships. It was dangerous work with the water breaking unpredictable on the rocks and shallows.

Word reached back to Francis and Perinella Delucette there son Felps on a risky dive pulled up a chest that was magically locked and was bringing it back to the academy to be unsealed. As Felps had slid the chest onto the longboat a wave hit that ground the two divers that had pulled it up with him under the boat on the rocks. Felps like taking risks and they had been friends, inspiring Felps to vow to use whatever was in the chest so the price they paid would not be in vain. He spent the next three days sleeping with a bottle of rum as the ship made its way back around the coast and the remainder of the journey recovering from his binge.

The affairs of the academy did not pause while they awaited the arrival of their son. Perinella sometimes wished they could slow down a little, Francis was glad they were always too busy.

"I still wish he would not take such risks." Perinella stated exasperated. "He can hire divers to do the dangerous work and it is still his claim."

"He loves the thrill of the dive. It would be wrong if we tried to steal him away from the work he loves. Besides he has enough magic to escape anything life threatening to himself." Francis dismissed her worry

158

for the seventh time.

"I would argue, but I have to get to this class, we are getting twenty-five gold pieces a head for five days of training and there are twelve members of the crew. They are not the sharpest wits we have taught but I am sure I can get them doing at least basic cantrips."

Francis chuckled, "Have fun with that." and walked out headed towards their private docks. They were barely more floating wharfs that you could tie small boats to, nothing more than five people could row up with. The water was also too shallow for any serious boats to get close. It served their purposes though, local boating without paying docking fees and they could slip small cargo in without dealing with port authority or having it inspected.

The ship was parked in sight of their private dock, but not of the main port for Kelleeshia. Francis could see Felps in the longboat with its meager crew as they rowed up to the dock and reached them about the time they were done getting tied off. All four crewmen transferred the chest from the boat to a small cart on the wharf.

"That is a sizable chest, Felps." Francis called out.

"With a strong magical seal like that I am sure it does not just contain gold or mundane precious items. I figure we can open it in the round room at the rear of the academy."

"We'll get it cleaned off so we can read any inscriptions or warnings before we decide on opening it." Francis motioned the crewmen to pause as the cart came beside him. He took the base of his staff and knocked barnacles off the circular medallion on the top of the chest. He ran his hand through his beard in thought. "There are old stories of legend that whisper of lost artifacts from before the Dragons brought life to this world. That could be an emblem from legend. Where did you find this chest, on a boat?"

"Not really." Felps looked closer at the round emblem. "This chest was wedged in the stone below the cliffs. It looked like it had been there much longer than the ships and the stone had grown around it."

"Or perhaps buried in legendary times in solid rock because of the greatness of value and only exposed by the ocean eating away at the rock." Excitement at the prospects fill his eyes as Francis wave the crewmen to continue and followed with Felps.

*   *   *   *

*

Lyamy sat Freyie in the shallow water of the beach as she watched the children of their den playing in the ocean waves. She smiled as she watched, "You know Freyie, they will never grasp the concept of not being able to play as children. Even though they will be able to look at our memories and see we did not have the freedom they have, it will be a detached concept."

"I try to forget those times myself." Freyie commented. "Even though it was not that long ago, it feels like it was another lifetime."

Lyamy laughed. "It really was as far as the clan knew we all died, or we would not have gotten away. So much has changed ..."

160

Lyamy broke off mid-sentence. Shadows of events to come danced in her mind. Humanoids with painted skin, yet not painted blotted random coloring no real pattern. Violence as they appeared from the middle of battle rampaging before they knew they were here. She could not place where the event would happen. The event was clear but the location was shadowed as if yet undetermined. Somehow, she knew they would become her friends, but events around that were even clouded.

Whatever was happening, there were ripples in the flow of time. She saw what looked to be ancient threads of time so old but beginning new again in the flow of events. Whatever was coming was having effects in the wake of its arrival like rain before a storm. Scattered raindrops of time appeared in the threads and waves around the world and maybe beyond.

"... Lyamy, are you alright. ... Hello Lyamy." The voice of Freyie was reaching through her vision. She used the voice to pull herself back. "You are back, good! Where were you? You literally started to fade." Freyie was holding her by the shoulder concern etched in her eyes.

"I am so sorry, Freyie. I am anchored in at least one other place but thank you for pulling me back." Lyamy shook her head. "I will have to consult ShadowDancer on that vision." Lyamy turned and pointed to an odd plant growing in the beach like it has been there all along. "The rain drops of time threads. There is a powerful, although sloppy event of magic cascading through the events of time."

Freyie looked at the plant Lyamy was pointing to. While it did not look totally out of place on a beach with large fronds and what looked like a fruit bulb of some kind in the middle, she had never seen one before. "Where did that come from?"

"Be careful we know nothing about that plant. I think it is from Ethar, the question is more when did it come from? Something disturbed a large, bundled time thread in the very long ago past. Something else restoring that bundle in the near future. Soon enough that we are starting to see a speckling of threads falling out ahead of the rest of the bundle." Lyamy shrugged, "I am probably not making sense, but I have no better way to explain what I am seeing." Lyamy tossed a shell from the beach into the fronds of the plant. The fronds where the shell hit curled as if spring loaded wrapping the shell and pulling it into the core of the plant. The plant was big enough to capture a large animal or beast.

"It eats things that get caught in it?" Freyie looked horrified. That is dangerous on the beach here, the children and other people need to be warned."

"I will move this for now, but we are going to see a lot of other things we do not recognize appearing at random. We need to alert everyone." Lyamy used the magics she knew to move the plant to an island she had discovered to the north that was uninhabited. They gathered the children and headed into the sanctuary. Lyamy lagged behind long enough to divide herself into another copy of herself and then caught up.

Alone on the beach she closed her eyes and a moment later she was in the place where ShadowDancer gave sanctuary to her messengers.

162

She stepped up to ShadowDancer and bowed her head slightly in respect. "Ancient ShadowDancer, I have become aware of a major time event colliding with us in the near future. You are probably already aware."

"I know something is happening, but very little about it. I have seen that it effects the threads of time but did not see it as a time event. An army is being brought into this world from somewhere and it is a fixed event that it will happen, but the location was not at all clear."

"It is not from somewhere; it is from the past. A time event from the legendary past is looping back into the near future. It is not well contained, and we have random things falling out from the coming event. A plant appeared on the beach near Freyie and I. I can see that there are scattered events happening everywhere. They will build to the big event and taper off after."

"You have seen some of this more clearly than I have." ShadowDancer smiled, "I hoped you would see it on your own, but I had no idea. We need to share information now. I would like to have you available to be at which ever location this army is brought through. There will be a lot of destruction before they realize they have been pulled out of their war."

They pooled their knowledge. Lyamy was surprised to learn she could see more of the time events then ShadowDancer although ShadowDancer could see more of the consequential events. Between the two of them they started working on getting a clearer picture of what to expect.

*

Corvuset could sense he was once again that the Ancients who had overpowered him were gone from the southern kingdoms again. That avatar was too powerful to be just an avatar, she had more power than he did. He was alone again now and bound only to the rules he was supposed to be following anyway. She had dominating control over him and could use him like a puppet, but was giving him total freedom, almost encouraged him to continue his subterfuge as long he did not overstep her intentions.

He assessed his situation now that he was calm. Very little was changed other then he could not personally act, he had to have his avatars or representatives act for him. He could not overthrow the current kingdom in Ehrbron at this time, but he could keep his underground organizations in full swing. He could orchestrate power and profiteering, even expand his operations. He would start with Rachette his Ehrbron boss. Make him his number one avatar and grant him a few tricks to help him rule the other bosses.

There were seven kingdoms and another dozen plus villages where his guilds ran the crime syndicates. In some cases that meant they ran the politicians that ran everything else also. Activity sanctioned by the guilds and those involved were under some protection by the guilds. Outsiders could find some shelter as long as they registered and paid their dues. Any criminal activities performed outside of guild authority had more to worry about from the syndicates then from the law.

Corvuset left his private sanctuary and appeared in the warehouse in Ehrbron. "Rachette, I am making you my first avatar. It is time to establish our new order of operations."

"I thought those lady ancients were shutting down your operations?" his boss replied.

"Not at all, thwarted planes of overthrowing the kingdom, and required I abide by the rules of the accord. Other than that she has, or they have allowed me to continue the rest of our plans and operation. Something to do with giving people choices to determine their own paths."

"So, what does being your avatar means that is different from being your boss in Ehrbron?"

"You will be my 'First' avatar, the rest will answer to you. The bosses from the other guilds halls may also be promoted to avatars, but they will still answer to you." Corvuset placed a hand on Rachette's shoulder.

"More responsibility and authority. I can work with that. Can I take a cut of their operations?"

"And my friend a little power to help you establish your position." A small surge passed from Corvuset to Rachette. "You will find that all your skills have been improved enough to give you more of an edge. Your senses are sharper now. I have granted you a few other abilities you will find useful for the job. Focus on Delphia the boss from Brookhaven and etched in the air a symbol that looks like the number two with a tail going straight down."

Rachette did as he was instructed and Delphia appeared in front of him pulling a piece of bread she had just taken a bite out of from her mouth. "Where, How …." disorientation had her at a loss for words.

"Hello Delphia, you are going to be my number two avatar."

She turned and saw Corvuset and that seemed to explain everything to her. "You summoned me. She nodded with a slightly quirked smile."

"Actually, Rachette did. He has been given the position of my number one avatar, in charge of all operations throughout the southern kingdoms."

"I work for him?" She eyed Rachette with some degree of disdain.

"You work for me." Corvuset stated with simple coolness. "He is the primary coordinator of activity for me now, so you answer to him."

She bowed her head slightly acknowledging her instructions. Corvuset had Rachette summon all the bosses one at a time. He granted each some elevated ability and the ability to return to their separate headquarters from any location. Training and instruction lasted several hours, long enough that he provided them all a meal. After the meal he presented them with an overview of the general plans of operation.

Delphia took opportunity when they were done to ask about something that had happened in Bookhaven. "Earlier today, out of nowhere a large lizard appeared in the middle of town. It was a variety no one recognized, although it was bigger than a horse. There are also rumors of other strange things appearing from rock formations to plants. Do you have anything to do with these occurrences?"

A general murmuring of similar inquiries occurred. They all had reports of these types of events. Corvuset for the first time though maybe he could benefit from this connection he had to Lyamy. "I was not aware of these incidents. Give me a moment to see if I can learn anything about them." In his mind he projected his thoughts to Lyamy asking if she knew anything about these events. He turned back to his bosses. "Apparently there is something big happening soon causing these small events to occur like a shower sprinkling before a big storm. A collision of a time event. Report back all information about these events that you can gather."

The number of incidents they documented before breaking up was significant, but still relatively scattered. Corvuset was not even sure they were all related as he went through their notes with Rachette. There were very strange sudden appearances like a three-foot circle of swamp appearing in the middle of a rock shelf or a purple mist appearing and dissipating. Corvuset was not going to discount any item even if it looked to him as if it was an ordinary event.

Pausing in the middle of their review Corvuset looked at Rachette and felt something he did not remember ever feeling before. He was not alone Rachette was his avatar, and more than just a tool. He did not have to hide from all other Ancients, he worked with others now, well maybe for them, but with them. He had asked them for information, and they gave it to him. He was a part of something bigger than himself he belonged somewhere, and he would keep them hidden, but he actually had feelings. Life had become more then an abstract concept of manipulation.

*   *   *   *

*

Lyamy sat on the parapet looking inward over the Shadow Valley. Pterdin was keeping her company. Lyamy was experiencing really mixed feelings. "It seems, Pterdin, as if the more I see and know, the more it feels like I will never get to see or know. Like the people that live in the village bellow us. They have ordinary lives with a hustle and excitement for their lives, but I will never know what it would be like to live like that. I only know that I will not know because coming here I know more then I knew before."

Pterdin tilted his head sideways and looked at her. "Here you can be in more than one place at the same time, you can experience different things at the same time, you can share the experiences of those you have linked with and you are worried about the things you may not experience? If I give you a present with a beautiful gift in a box would you open the box and wonder what could have fix in the empty space or would you appreciate the gift?"

Lyamy laughed. "I did not mean it like that, of course I would appreciate the gift. I meant more like, if you live in a box and all you know is the box, you feel like you know almost all there is, but when you discover there is a world outside your box, the more you learn the more you know there is to learn. Sometimes it feels a little overwhelming to try

168

to imagine just how much is out that I am yet to learn."

"To most you at fourteen are still a child and you have had more change happen in the last year than most people see in a lifetime. It is alright to feel a little overwhelmed. You should talk about it like you are not though, it helps keep things in perspective. It would probably do both of you good if you and ShadowDancer were to talk about these things together. She has never really had anyone to confide in as a peer."

"Pterdin, I have a question for you."

"Alright, you know leading into a questions like that builds tension before the question is even asked."

"Sorry, I am just curious. You are supposed to keep track of me, but I am in more than one place at a time and can project another presence at any time anywhere I want, I think. How can you keep track of everything I do to make sure I don't step out of bounds?"

Pterdin laughed. "First, I am not your keeper, I am an observer and adviser. Second, I too can be in more than one place even as you, one of the reasons I was picked. Now add to that, we share a link, and I know even as your den knows where you are if not what you are doing. I am sure if you were to start hiding things form me, I might ask you why."

"It is approaching mid-day; I should head to our designated meeting place. I assume you are going to continue with us as you have invisible. We are getting teleported to Kelleeshia."

"Don't worry you will not lose me." Pterdin snickered and vanished.

They met at the front gates to ShadowKeep. The mercenaries were there and Lyamy gave them a generous retainer for future services. They would be headed back to Ehrbron. Captain Brandon had been shown the certificates of full pardon from the king for both families. He would keep that information secret until they were separated on their different paths.

The women and youngsters were there when Lyamy arrived. Martin showed up moments later with a backpack and a second bag he was carrying. "Had to get samples to try and find markets where we are going. If I am successful, we will be able to collect a small commission on sales. I really think the red rock carving will be a popular item."

"With your ingenuity and imagination I am surprised you were not successful in Ehrbron in keeping some profitable business going." Lyamy nodded her approval.

"Ah, but there I had to get through government permits and approvals for every change and with successful approval in that venue, I still have to get protection approval and pay a percentage to the guilds touched by anything I did. After a while there is a point where you start losing money when business gets better dealing with all those cutthroat organizations to stay in business."

"That should be changing. If what I have done works, both sides government and organized crime are going to be more interested in the success of business then draining them out of existence." Lyamy gave a confident smile. "They have more to gain from prosperity now then from hardship."

"Who has more to gain?" Micheal asked as he walked up with a new tradesman bag filled with smithy tools. "I figured I should have the tools of my trade if I am going to have any chance of earning my way as we go and providing for my family. There are some very interesting developments here I picked up on too. It seems they use some hinge designs brought here by their leader HonorLord along with other mechanisms with some fine detailed parts that I have not seen in other places. I have never met gnomes myself but based on stories I would imagine some of these devices might be of their design."

The gathering or the traveling companions was complete and ShadowDancer appeared with her brother and sister. "Franklin and Roxanne are in training they will send you to Kelleeshia. You will find yourselves just out of sight of the gates when you appear so as not to cause any alarm. Captain Brandon we can send you back to the border of Ehrbron territory if you would like."

"That would save us a long ride. You have been more then generous to us." He turned to Lyamy, "We are at your call whenever you need us." Then back to ShadowDancer, "We are ready."

ShadowDancer gave Franklin a nod and the mercenary unit vanished. "Well done, Franklin. If you have any questions Lyamy just let me know."

"I will. I believe we are also ready." Lyamy noted she could teleport her companions on her own, but ShadowDancer seemed to be working with her brother and sister to get them familiar with what they were doing. The two families were huddled together and from what Lyamy could sense they were much happier than they had been in a long time.

ShadowDancer nodded to Roxanne and with a momentary blur they found themselves off to the side of a road, with the walls of Kelleeshia in sight. As they took the few steps to the road, the gates came into full view.

"This place dwarfs Ehrbron." Micheal stated looking at the city wall that vanished in both directions, blending with the terrain as it reaches far enough to make it impossible to see the difference. "Perhaps even bigger than ShadowKeep although that place is much bigger on the inside."

Lyamy nodded, "It is bigger than ShadowKeep, but not bigger than Shadow Valley. You are correct though Shadow Valley has secrets that make it much larger than the space it occupies. There is a tavern on the main street as we enter town called simple Kelleeshia's Bed and Breakfast. It is the first tavern built here, although it has been rebuilt a few times. We will meet in the restaurant there in three days. Once we are inside the gates, I have business I need to take care of and you are free to take care of the business you have or just see the city. If you run into trouble just call for me with your thoughts."

"You can hear our thoughts?" Mathew asked.

"If you call for me I will here you, that is different from hearing everything you think."

"Should we rent a room there?" Janice asked.

"You can, it may make things easier. If you turn right on the street just after the tavern, three blocks down on the right is a much less expensive hostel of good reputation. That will also shelter you from being labeled rich tourists."

"Any suggestions for finding our way around town?" Martin asked.

"If you are willing to pay the modest fee you can hire one of the rickshaws to take you around town for the day. They know the city so anything you want to find they can help. You can probably commission one for the full three days for a gold or two. Also, a generous tip may get you in doors you might not otherwise find."

"You have been here before." Kara stated as if revealing a great secret.

"I have and I learned that these people really care about their money. It is almost a game they play the endless exchange of money and goods or services."

The guards at the gate asked them about their intent and business in Kelleeshia. They stopped their search and questioning as soon as Lyamy stated she had business with Magus Kremlern. Her name was on his list so anyone with her had unobstructed access. She parted company with the others in front of the tavern they would meet again later. She divided herself projecting the division to Mathew's home in Ehrbron and the other heading to speak with the Magus.

*   *   *   *

*

Their library was probably the most extensive when it came to the knowledge of the time of legends. This meant in the opinion of Francis Delucette that they knew nothing, and the rest of the world knew less. "This is the seal of one of their powerful entities that they worshiped based on what has been understood. I can barely give you a loose interpretation of the glyphs that underscore here. Something to the effect of what was, is or will be done, or cast, cannot or will not, maybe has not been undone. Then something about great power."

"Great power?" Felps said with excitement. "I knew treasure hunting would pay off. Let's open it and see what is inside."

"That is a warning Felps! Warning precedes bad things happening. Be patient, we will evaluate what we can see with magic first. Yes, at some point we will open it and since it is your prize, we will let you do whatever part you can." Francis turned away. "For now, I am going to go back in and have dinner. Don't lag too long, you know Perinella hates it if you wait until food is cold before eating." He strolled to the door grabbing his staff leaning by the door on the way out.

Felps circled the chest several times and stopped in what he interpreted as the front. Where you might expect a clasp and lock on most chests there was an inset with an image. Looking closely, it seemed familiar to him. The top half had what could be seen as a sun and clouds, but the bottom the moons and stars. On the left the top swirled into the bottom and on the right the bottom swirled into the top like someone had twisted it slightly counterclockwise while it was wet. It was deliberately carved that way in the stone though. It was also in reverse relief,

He had seen a stone with the image reversed. Felps realized the stone he had used as a paperweight was a perfect match for the impression on the chest. Felps went to his office and returned several minutes later with the stone. The stone looked like a perfect fit, the back was smooth, with nothing to get a grip on once he placed it into the chest. No operating instructions and it was a stone he had discovered years before he started his treasure hunting. It had been in a miscellaneous pile of junk when he was going to the Kremlern academy as a child. It had no detectable magic and came from the age of legends. As he brought it into the room with the chest, he felt it coming to life in his hand.

Felps no longer knew if he was doing things because he wanted to, or if these artifacts were controlling his actions. The non-magical stone he had from childhood pulsed with power in his hand and it felt good. It was not arcane power, and he did not know what it was. Movement became distorted almost as if what he was seeing was moving at different rates in time. He stepped towards the chest and he was there. Kneeling down he held the stone in his palm and pressed it into place. The distortions around him cleared instantly and he looked at what he had done.

The chest opened slowly revealing the contents inside the stone box. There was a large orb one pedestal in the middle and a collection of other objects, rings, amulets, wands and random trinkets, around the orb. It appeared to be a black sphere filled with continuous movement on the inside that you could feel more then see looking at it. It was in a golden podium obviously designed to support the dark orb.

"Felps what are you doing?" Francis yelped as he stepped in with Perinella on his heals. "We were going to study the warning before opening that thing. You could have brought destruction on all of us."

"You did something already, there was a random rippling of time distortions. We do not know the consequences of what you have done already." Perinella stated with a chilling coldness.

"I don't know what I did." Felps stated honestly. "I remember the impression on the chest looked like if fit my paperweight. I felt so much time pass and yet as if no time had passed at all, then the chest was open, and I was staring deep into that orb."

"This has taken a strong influence on your thinking. Let's get out of this room so we can talk about it with clear heads." Francis grabbed Felps by the shoulder and pulled him back out through the door they came in. Perinella pushed Felps to keep him moving.

"I must hold that dark orb, it is my destiny to activate the power within. It is why I received the key to the chest so long ago and only I survived the retrieval. I was called from the time of legends." Felps sounded slightly out of control.

"Sit down here and eat your dinner. Maybe you will make more sense on a full stomach." Perinella commanded Felps with the tone of her voice.

"Do you remember unlocking the chest?"

"It is hazy, but I think so. Francis, my stone fit perfect into the chest and the chest opened on its own. It feels like so much happened that I don't remember, like I went back to when the chest was first sealed. I was given instructions and I have to follow them. When it is time, that which was done must be finished."

"Well, you are not going to activate that thing in the same city I live in if you are not going to wait for us to understand what we are doing first." Perinella was insistent. "You can take it to a remote location, like the forbidden continent or somewhere away from us."

*   *   *   *

*

King Tagmerian was reading through a handful of complaints and suggestions from the people. With the implementation of the prosperity packages, he had started gaining favor with his people, both military and civilian. He had listened to Lyamy when she was there and decided to invest in ways to help his people prosper and grow in their ability to bring money into Ehrbron through trade and productive means. His own people could have made the swords he ordered from the northern continent and that was a new change. Thirty blacksmiths had work for at least a year now just making swords. Some blacksmiths were working on armor and it would take about six months to train additional young apprentices to the point they could shift some of the workload enough for more to start work on armor.

Money in the hands of these families boosted food markets and other resource suppliers for family use goods. Money also flowed from business to business, the blacksmiths needed supplies of metal and coal and materials to run their business. Other craftsmen were put to work doing repair work to buildings. Just this one business pursuit within the city and kingdom stimulated a large quarter of the economy.

The second effort towards stimulating prosperity was to reface the streets and public buildings. Repairs and refinishing provided continuous work and generated the same rippling growth to the community. After seeing the almost instant boost to the community from the first week King Tagmerian ordered that any business that can possibly be done with services and purchasing from within the kingdom by any official capacity was to be done internally.

He ordered anonymous suggestions boxes to be placed to get feedback from the people. It seemed everyone was still hesitant to put anything in the boxes, but there were a few. He was very interested in what they had to say, if there was anything constructive and he wanted to see how the messages changed over time. So, while the numbers were small, he would take the time to read them all himself. He may have to bring a team in to read and sort them later.

"You have a good start going here." Lyamy said as she appeared seated in a chair to his right at the table where he was reading.

"Perhaps I will leave a legacy for restoring the kingdom and bringing a season of peace." He did not seem surprised at her arrival and the guards at the door returned to their posts when they realized who it was. "History has been cruel to the southern kingdoms; and until you started haunting me, I was carrying on the same practices as my fathers and blind to other possibilities.”

“You have never married and have no offspring of your own.” Lyamy was obviously leading into something.

“I saw no reason to continue the saga of a cruel line of Kings who offered nothing better then the people would have if they were occupied by a neighboring kingdom. These petty wars and feuds have never served the people well. There did not seem to be a point in continuing a line of Kings that everyone hated. Now, well, my season for producing an heir has passed. I can leave the Kingdom better then I received it though.”

“Do you remember I had you sign pardons for a couple families last time we met?”

“Yes, Laymy I do. Although I trusted you and did not even read them.”

“I think it would serve you well if upon their return you took them under your roof and cared for the one boy as if he were your nephew. If all goes well, you may even select him as a chancellor to rule over your nobles as heir. That will be up to you when the time comes. Your gatekeeper of the future.”

“Who is this young man?”

“His name is Mathew. His father is a blacksmith learning to refine his skills in other lands. He would be a good candidate for a Royal Blacksmith.”

“And this other family, why should I give care to them.”

"Martin is a very good Merchant. Even now he is setting up trade arrangements between different lands, receiving a small commission from every exchange he has arranged. If you put him in charge of appropriations for the realm, I am sure he would keep things managed avoiding waste and serve you well in that capacity. They are civilians from Ehrbron who have seen the dark side of the kingdom and would give care to the people and the welfare of all."

"You have not steered me wrong yet. When will they return to the kingdom?"

"We are still weeks away from our goal and it does take time for these gentlemen to learn and manage the business at hand. Between six weeks and two months."

"Let me know when you are bringing them back."

"I will. For now, I need to see to a few other things before I am gone. Remember it is still your kingdom, but you can call on me if you need help." Lyamy slipped back into her maximum speed, vanishing to any who were looking at her and headed to the warehouse on the dock.

The open display of activity from the secured warehouse had increased. Corvuset's avatar Rachette was obviously not as concerned about secrecy as Corvuset had been. There was a shift in the operation also. It appeared to be more about protecting the business operations that paid and running a profitable business. Not to make the mistake of thinking there was any less thieving and cutthroat activity. That was still the cornerstone of the operation. However, the front end business at the warehouse was a fully legitimate operation they could hide behind.

Lyamy reached out with a thought and located Corvuset. He was actually in his own private sanctuary. It only took another thought, and she was with him. "Greetings, Corvuset. Forgive the intrusion." He had created a private world like all ancients did. She noticed that his seemed incomplete around the edges which seemed typical, and he had no outside world. He did however have the place heaped with lavish wealth.

"You who spared me and gave me a place and purpose I never before had. You are always welcome to visit. I suspect this is more business though then a social visit."

Lyamy laughed. "I will let you decide that. I just thought I would drop by and let you know I am impressed with how quickly operations have turned around in Ehrbron. I am sure you find the advantages of not having to be there all the time making things happen. I have not made a place of my own yet, well nothing more than a workout room anyway."

"I know you are ShadowDancer's avatar, but I think you also know you have stepped beyond that and have become an Ancient in your own right."

"I know. I am destined even as you are to be on ShadowDancer's council of Ancients. We all represent different aspects of life and choices people make. Those choices are not always that clear and distinct so there are greater complications then say good and evil. You are not just stealing killing and mischief, you empathize with the downcast and desperate, those who live under a cloak using whatever means possible to survive.

You just happen to favor the shall we say less upstanding methods in the eyes of good society."

"You read me well. You probably know I am not pleased that Rachette has put himself out where he can be easily discovered by the curious. He should have stooges out there, but it is his choice. Delphia is earning more of my favor, she even conceals her thoughts from herself at times."

"It is your tapestry to weave how your followers perceive you. Just as it is their interaction that will weave the tapestry of their lives and the future of their people. What more of these random events have been reported by your people?"

"Well, most appear to be harmless appearances ranging from two to six feet in diameter when they occur. The size seems to be dependent upon what is appearing almost like things being teleported but depending on their size it is a bubble that includes a piece of their environment. Something the size of a fly might be totally missed, where something the size of a person would be about a six-foot bubble. There have been no half creatures or parts of objects cut by the edge of the bubble."

"Any unique objects? I mean I had a plant come through about fifteen feet from where I was sitting, and it would eat any object that fell against its fronds. There have been some reports of other objects like a stone signpost and a pile of clothing."

"There is detail in the reports I have gotten that I have not read. Honestly, I was looking to try and see if there was any pattern to the

182

locations. Nobody has died yet that I am aware of from any of these things coming through. So far the only creatures that have come through seem to be wild beasts that have run off."

"The events will become more frequent, then something big is going to happen, then they will taper off. I am guessing that if we were to study this, we might find these events have been occurring for a very long time, just with a low enough frequency not to catch our attention." Lyamy stood up, she had learned what she was looking for, still no solid evidence supporting the things they have seen looking ahead. "We need to look for anything that will tell us where these events are coming from. Anything that may indicate intelligence or culture."

"So, this was really mostly a social visit. You have no fear of coming to me in my space even though I tried to kill you. Not only that you have taken me into the fold where you serve."

"I have nothing to fear. You have no intention of trying to harm me again, I can sense that, but even if you wanted, you could not. If you wish to test it try. The bond you are under will not allow you to cause me harm."

"Seriously, you are saying I cannot even slap you?" Corvuset had no real desire to hurt Lyamy, but to find out she had him in a bond that would stop any attempt was enough to arouse his curiosity.

"You cannot take action to hurt me. Go ahead and try if you need to see if it is true." Lyamy stood there an easy target for anything he wanted to try.

Corvuset swung his hand, and it came well short of striking her. He looked at his arm and tried again but got no closer. "So, I cannot strike you." He made a gesture, and a book flew off a shelf behind her, but it too missed. "How does that work? I am prevented from doing anything that will cause you harm also." He really did not expect an answer.

Lyamy knew the loopholes in the bond but was not about to share them. "It is a bond I learned from the primordial magic I was trained in when I was young, but I have learned to apply it with other forms of power. I placed the bond on you as a defensive measure, after all you did try to kill me. I am sure if I had not you would not still be around, ShadowDancer does not like bad things to happen to me."

"I do not understand why you did not want me eliminated after what happened. For that matter I still have no idea how you are still alive without getting help from someone else. I know you cannot tell me that secret."

"I learned a long time ago the value of turning an enemy into a friend. Will I ever forget what you did?" Lyamy pulled her shirt back exposing the scar on her shoulder and chest. "I do not want to forget. You taught me not to trust Ancients I do not know. Why would I want you dead when I can now see your every thought if I want to and make you do anything I wish." She pushed her will on him and he raised his hand then he placed it flat on the table. She pushed her mind into him a little further and with her speed and accuracy he pulled his dagger and planted it in the wooden table between his thumb and first finger. Then she pulled back and let him go. "You see. I really do own you. You have freedom because I choose to let you have freedom."

Corvuset looked at her and visibly shook. "You are more terrifying than I ever dreamed of being. I could feel the savage beast when you controlled me. I suspect what I did to you was civilized compared to what you are capable of doing."

"You have nothing to fear, you are a friend now." Lyamy laughed. "Unless you choose not to be, it is not required. In the eyes of the people of Ehrbron you are my enemy and that is good for them to think that way. The influences of others will come also, and the people will build us into what they think we should be and right or wrong use us to justify their choices."

"I don't know if the game you are playing is better or worse than the old games of the Ancients." Corvuset poured a glass of nectar from a bottle that appeared as he reached for it into a glass that appeared as he held it up. Lyamy accepted the offer and waited for him to pour his own before taking a sip. "They pitted their races and developments against each other and waged wars or bid for power. The races knew who they were and where they stood. They knew who they served and were not plagued with figuring out their own fate. You and ShadowDancer I suppose present us with a new game of influence, twisting our influences into mixed societies that do not all follow after the same Ancient, allowing the people to make their choices with guidance not direction."

"If I had been directed, you would be dead. Instead, you will sit on the council of ShadowDancer. If I had directed King Tagmerian the change would have been too drastic for the people to believe and possibly less successful. He still has his hunger for power and his mighty army that can keep the lesser kingdoms at bay. Without you forcing their hand, your people may still push towards rebellion or they may secure a stronger footing in the underground with splinter factions running their covert operations against covert operations."

Corvuset smile a wry plotting smile. "If I reward Delphia it will promote competition between avatars for favor which will keep the edge in play throughout the organization."

"Ah yes, intrigue a venue that has become a part of you out of necessity to survive and yet Rachette is in the perfect position to spread your influence through the trade routes and other kingdoms."

"You managed to avoid the question about your survival. An Ancient cannot even survive being sliced into two pieces, split through the heart. I know I saw the body parts there as you slid apart. Only instead of fear your eyes filled with anger."

"It did hurt, and you did not miss. You are correct it was me not a construct. If you ask the Nine Sisters, her secret will she tell you? If you ask Gaharias how the first elves received the power they were born with, will he tell you? Are there any secrets you have that you simply will not willingly share? I am not avoiding your question; I simply choose not to answer."

"Fair enough I suppose, although apparently I can have no secrets

186

from you."

"I am not going to look unless you give me reason to look. Seriously this is not the first time I have used this bond. I am sure there are at least a few things in there I really do not even want to know." Lyamy finished her glass and set it down on a table that wasn't there leaving the glass floating in the air. "So that is the nectar of the Ancients. It is pleasant to drink. Thank you for your hospitality, but I must be on my way."

"It was actually pleasant having you stop by." Corvuset finished his drink also. Lyamy vanished from his presence. He could feel the departing presence of the Ancient.

*   *   *   *

*

Lyamy was intercepted on her way to the Magus and caught in a moment with ShadowDancer and Eric. "Lyamy, forgive me for pulling you from what you were doing. I want you to be in every location we have discuss as possible areas for the major time event collisions." ShadowDancer glanced back at Eric.

"I strain with four locations at a time. Thirteen will be hard to focus." Lyamy looked a little flustered.

"We have to expand your mental capacity to accommodate the accomplishing this task. Which is why I have asked Eric, my father to assist." ShadowDancer gently moved her between them. "After this you will find yourself a full-fledged Ancient, receiving requests and able to answer. There are also a couple locations we can remove from the thirteen.

Glimpses of time threads have cleared them."

"Erhbron can be removed also." Lyamy stated. "Even though the shadows of the time event collision had suggested the possibility none of the future threads for those of Erhbron that I have seen show a hint of any repercussions."

"I can agree with that." ShadowDancer nodded. "This means you will only need to be in nine places at the same time."

"Ten if I am still traveling when the event occurs."

"Ten." Eric agreed. "We are going to expand what you are. You are being trusted, by us, with more power than most of the Ancients of Ethar. If I read what the barriers are telling me correctly, they endorse what we are about to do. We will only do this if you agree. You have been through changes already, so you have some idea what to expect. ShadowDancer went through the change naturally, it was a part of her when she was born. I went through the change at a much later age, born mortal and without power. I cannot think of any reason you would oppose. Are you ready?"

"I accept the responsibility as ShadowDancer has seen fit for me. I have not been steered wrong that I know of, so Yes, I am ready."

ShadowDancer placed a hand on her shoulder. Lyamy felt layers of expansion in her mind. The sensation of doors opening, growing in depth and breadth. Her separate selves became more clearly defined in her mind, easier to keep uniquely focused. She felt as if she was becoming more aware of the world and the universe around her. She could feel the sun, moons, planets she did not know existed. She pulled herself back. She could feel everything around her from bugs to rocks in the ground and the deeper substance of things she thought she knew before.

"Lyamy?" Eric's voice pierced her explorations. Seeing he had her attention he continued. "You do not need to explore everything now; you will have plenty of time for that when we are done. We need to focus on what is here at least until after the time collision event."

Lyamy sent out her multiplicities. "Elven, one to stay with you." She bowed her head slightly to ShadowDancer in acknowledgment of her authority.

She paused in her tracks. The moment was released, she with ShadowDancer. She was already with the Magus now also, so she no longer needed to go there. She turned and headed back to the tavern; she was the traveling companion copy. She would explain to the Magus that she would be searching the other houses for anyone who may be orchestrating the coming event. Her time senses told her it was orchestrated a long time ago and current events would be no more than an unfolding of what was already done. However, if they could identify the current actors in the puzzle, they might be able to control some of the outcome. She rented a room at the Tavern and headed back out.

*   *   *   *

*

Something dark was moving deep below the water. Rachette could feel it but had no clue what he was feeling so he chose to ignore it. It was alive though. She opened her eyes. She was in two pieces; she could feel it as she adjusted to seeing what was around her. She brushed away the small fish that were picking at her and pulled the two pieces back together. There was no heartbeat, but how could there be it was cut in half. She was a construct of darkness, anger, fear, hate, these were the things she was made from. She used the cut and torn garments she had to tie herself back together. She would find a better way later.

She drank in the anger and hate, the negative energy from the city above fed her power. Who was she, she was having trouble remembering? She had been cut in half; she could still feel the searing pain as the blade sliced through her. She was Lyamy, but she was not Lyamy. She did not know how she came to be, but she was, and she fed on dark energy. No heartbeat and no breath, she moved through the water with ease. She needed clothing and something to hold herself together better then tied pieces of tattered cloth. She felt the anger of a tailor sewing some leather garment, they would have clothing and thread to sew her back together. With a slight twitch of thought, the tailor slipped and drove the needle into their hand. The burst of rage made the location easy to find.

She locked the doors and closed the blinds with a thought when she entered the shop. She could feel the tailor in the back cleaning her wound. She had lots of anger and delicious dark feelings. The dark creature slipped into the back room with the shopkeeper unnoticed. The leather straps rose up and bound the ankles and wrists of the poor angry woman and pulled her flat against the wall. The ends of the straps merged into the wall binding her in place. Fear another delicacy filled her eyes.

190

The creature that was not Lyamy drank in the flavor.

She knew thoughts that had belonged to this Lyamy from before her death. Ancients? Creatures so young do not know what Ancient means. Memories awakening of a time of destruction. The wonderful feast of the pains of a dying world and time to sleep until new life returns with enough power to awaken the death changeling. This Lyamy had enough power that her pain had caused the awakening. These other creatures were too weak to have pulled her from her sleep. They had strong anger and fear though and this would feed her back to full strength. This woman did not have emotional strength in pain, but fear and anger did come very strong.

She grabbed the thread and bloody needle from the counter and began sewing herself back together in front of the terrified woman. The pain felt good, and the fear from the woman with every stitch felt better. She would take her time and make sure every stitch came with the delicious reward of fear and anger. Death did not server her, with death came the end of the emotions wrapped around pain, fear and anger. One more strap of leather moved from the bench with a thought. No need to listen to the screaming or chance someone passing by in the alley behind the shop to hear anything. The strap pressed into her mouth, the ends pulling taut into the wall, also securing her head from moving about.

The Death Changeling could feel the fear coursing through the woman with each stitch she sewed in her flesh and with every change that touched her. She collected leather garments, starting with a corset which would help keep the two pieces together. She was stuck in the form of this

Lyamy for now but was starting to remember her real name Cadabriana. She summoned an Ancient bug her memories were returning. With a touch the creatures started scurrying about beneath the skin of the terrified woman. This would be a continuous source of food as she stepped out and blended into this sweet corrupt society.

Her color was much darker than the original Lyamy, she laughed when she realized she was a black cat. Calamity trailed behind her as a thought here or there caused things to break or collide resulting in pain and accidents, in many cases even fighting. Cadabriana was a dark creature from before the great destruction. From what she held of the mind of Lyamy she was from the time of legends, destroyed when the magic lords lost control of their reckless use of time magic. The dirt, the dead and Cadabriana survived. Her master and creator dead and gone in one of the time storms he was partly responsible for causing.

Cadabriana twisted two fingers and a plank on the boardwalk to her right snapped and splintered as a young kid jumped on it. The splintered wood of the plank jumped up at an angle still fastened to the under structure and caught the man chasing him just above the groin leaving him half hanging gored on the fibered splinters. The kid vanished and Cadabriana turned and walked through the wall of the building to her left feeling her power increasing with every burst of pain and discomfort.

She had no purpose other than feeding on pain and discomfort. She had the form of the being that died giving her life from her deep hibernation. The sweet savor that gave her birth in this new age. She probed the mind of this Lyamy, but there were thoughts she could not access. The creature had more power than some of the old magic lords. Cadabriana froze in her tracks. This Lyamy was not dead, that explained the limited access to her thoughts. Cadabriana realized she did not have the full freedom she thought when she awoke. The creature that woke her from the deep shadows had the power and authority to command her even as the magic lord that brought her into the world the first time.

Cadabriana would find a way to be free. For now, this Lyamy did not know what she had awaken. Cadabriana would hide in the shadows and wait and watch until she could find a way to defeat her new master before binding commands stopped her from being able to take such actions. She would be stuck in this shadow image of her new master until her master was dead. It was time to learn what she could, her purpose until the task was done, to find a way to bring Lyamy to an end.

*   *   *   *

*

She had not found any of the houses or academies in Kelleeshia that knew or were studying magics of a nature that could cause a time rift. There had been a couple time ripples while she was there that seemed centered in the city somewhere. There were temporal displacements, but that was happening every time there was an event no matter how small. Lyamy ran out of time before identifying anything she could see as the source or focus of the disruptions. The threads all pointed to the big event in the future without a specific physical location.

They were on the ship now headed for the northern continent. The only one among the traveling companions that got seasick was Martin. He turned green and lost his last meal on the deck but recovered immediately when Lyamy touched him on the shoulder. The rain of time events continued even out at sea she noticed although very little survived unless it was an actual sea creature of otherwise oceanic event that dropped through.

Looking at the thread and the scope of magical vision the rainfall of time events was actually an amazing display. The effects on the course of current events varied from virtually no impact to devastating. Lyamy reached out with her new abilities and realized that more of the scattered effects were happening in space outside the atmosphere and some were below the surface. She reported this to ShadowDancer and she said Eric would watch that for now they needed to stay focused on Ethar.

Lyamy looked ahead and saw the threads twisting together. There as something a little bigger then the general smaller events were going to collide in their path. Lyamy had already noted that the collision of events was not always gracious. She observed an underground collision where the ground did not displace, and a creature was suddenly dropped out of time into solid rock. Other times the time event replaced what was there displacing what it collided with back into the stream of time distortions. Other events still displaced what was where they arrived pushing it in every direction to clear the space for the arrival of the displaced elements.

Something was probing at her thoughts she felt it for a moment,

194

and it was gone. It felt like when she had someone dominated. The sensation seemed to come from Ehrbron, but somehow, she knew it was not Corvuset, nor the soldier or agents she knew she dominated. It felt almost like a ghost of herself. Lyamy brought her mind back to where she was.

"Captain veer east, we need to circle around something that is about to collide with the ocean."

"We are on course lady. We cannot just wander the ocean there are currents that will pull us much farther off then we might intend. This is not like pulling a wagon down a cobble street."

"Captain, if you do not do as I have suggested, I will have to move the ship over myself. We do not want to be at the place of this coming time displacement. It might be dangerous still staying as close as I would like to be able to observe what is coming."

"Are you supposed to be some kind of oracle or something?" The Captain was looking less then amused

Lyamy captured the moment. The Captains looked a little less confident when time stood still around him. "I do not really have time for long explanations right now. I am an Ancient and if I must, I will move the ship on my own, but I would prefer you simply steer us on a course to avoid calamity. You are part human, perhaps you are not familiar with the power of an Ancient."

"A wizard with a little experience can place a dream in the mind of a man."

"Then what, Captain will convince you without causing harm? Not that as an Ancient I should have need to prove myself. Perhaps something nice." She touched the hilt of his sword at his belt and the handle turned gold with a large red gem in the pummel. "Plated in gold not solid, you need to keep the virtue of the weapon."

"If it is still gold when I come out of this dream, I will deviate our course. I am not going to assume you are more than a good wizard however, but you have paid me a sufficient reward to be worth the delay."

"Done." Lyamy smiled and time resumed. "By the way, it is also now a flame blade. So you know, My name is Lyamy."

The Captain turned the ship deviating the course in accordance with her instructions. "I recon I shant use it to open a bottle of rum then." He smiled.

"Keep your eye to the left and you will see what we are avoiding in about ten minutes." Lyamy slipped down to the main deck where she could get an open view from the rail. As she looked out over the waves, she realized she was drawing the attention of the crew and passengers on deck.

One of the crewmen stepped up and asked, "What has your attention on the waves out there?"

"I am hoping nothing we need to worry about, but I am watching so I can protect the ship if we do need to worry." Suddenly a wave started forming from the center point of the collision. She placed a hand on the rail and the ship rose up ahead of the wave, stable to avoid the tossing about that would have otherwise occurred.

The crewman's jaw dropped in amazement. "You are an Ancient." He spoke in a whisper.

The gap in the ocean was filled almost as fast as it formed. The displaced water was replaced with more water and a very large water creature with three heads. The creature reeled about obviously disoriented and unsure as the return wave from the displacement crashed back against the newly occupied area. Smaller fish and creatures from both sides started floating to the surface as the chemical differences between the waters made them unfriendly to the occupants one way or the other. Lyamy could feel that others made the adjustments with ease.

The creature reared up in the water, Lyamy could feel it was angry and confused. It started moving towards the ship. The ship was the nearest thing it could see and and instincts said it was being attacked and nothing else was around to place the blame. All three heads turned in the direction it was moving. The head on the left spew forth fire well short of reaching the ship and the head on the right sprayed a mist in the air that sizzled as it hit the surface of the ocean.

Lyamy held out her hand and a blue transparent wall appeared curved as if part of a much larger bubble protecting the ship from the approaching creature. Lyamy did not want to kill the beast it was a victim of circumstances. The sea dragon collided with the barrier and reeled back. Both the fire and the acid spray were deflected and slid down the outside of the bubble. All three heads roared and shrieked with anger and frustration before turning and diving into the depths of the sea.

Lyamy rolled her palm and unseen to the others the bubble of protection that was centered on the ship formed beneath the water protecting them from any attack to the underside. All other activity on the ship had ceased and everyone was still looking at the bubble that has protected them from certain destruction. Lyamy was back with the Captain and patted him on the shoulder before anyone realized she had moved. "Back on course good Captain, we have a schedule to keep."

"Yes, of course. Forgive my impudence." The ship was back in the water and he barked commands to adjust the sails and turned the rudder returning to course.

"You have caused no offense, Captain. Do not be alarmed."

"It is an honor then, Lyamy, to have you on board." The Captain now had the utmost respect for Lyamy.

Lyamy's travel companions smiled as they watched the reaction of everyone on board to their group leader and friend. They had a sense of pride for who they were traveling with, but to Lyamy's pleasure remained modest about everything. She took the time to pull them all to the side and express her appreciation. The balance of the journey by sea to the city of Talmorg would be without incident.

*   *   *   *

*

She maintained the form of Chareece and not ShadowDancer at the castle of her parents in the Walled City of Talmorg. Much like her avatar the Ancient or goddess depending upon who called upon her maintained herself in multiple places. One difference was only a very few knew that Chareece and ShadowDancer were the same. The fact that she could be both at the same time in the same room helped her conceal this secret.

Her mother Queen Saphrine and her father as far as the world knew King Talmorg both knew her secrets. They raised her from birth as Chareece first born princess. When she came into power as an Ancient it was not as big a change as it might have been if she was not used to the awe and respect of the people as royalty. She continued to maintain her presence as part of the royal family and ShadowDancer was her secret identity. It felt now more like Chareece was her secret identity, but either way she was both.

She shared with her parents the events that were happening around Ethar, so they knew the ship coming in this afternoon had a passenger new to the ranks of the Ancients. They were prepared to receive her, but there was no fanfare setup for the arrival of the ship. If she was traveling in discretion, they did not want to stir up unwanted recognition. Chareece seemed a little more preoccupied to them than normal so they did not push the issue for information either. The strange random time events were happening throughout the land and this also preoccupied their time making sure protection was provided.

Chareece had told them she was traveling with two families under her protection, so arrangements were made for them to stay in the palace complex while they were passing through. Escorts were set to meet them at the dock and show them anywhere they wanted and to let them know they have a place to stay in the palace as honored guests.

They arrived in the height of the day's activity. Lyamy was impressed the city was as big or bigger then Kelleeshia. There was a lot of magic used here also although more natural magic was employed. Unlike Kelleeshia the core population was elf instead of human although both cities were filled with a diverse population of mixed races. The populations mixed but did seem to group a little more by race here than they did in Kelleeshia. Humans also seemed to be the common factor in groups that were mixed races.

Activity in the city ranged from high intensity aggressive in-depth exchanges to perfunctory and mundane tasks. With the diversity of people in their gregarious activity came a multiplicity of moods and passions, although here they seemed to reflect a more positive and uplifted feeling. They were all glad to have their feet on solid ground again. Martin was as anxious to explore the merchant districts as Micheal was to meet the smiths and craftsmen. They did wait until they were shown their rooms and their families were settled in before vanishing until sunset.

Lyamy was almost immediately taken to meet the King and Queen and after the formal occasion slipped away with Chareece. "Your appearance is significantly different. If I did not know already, I may not have recognized you as ShadowDancer. Have you dabbled with changing your appearance to generate separate identities?"

Chareece smiled with a royal nod. "It is good to have your fresh new point of view on things. No, I have not, but I bet we could. I was never taught what we could or could not do when I came to power and I stumbled upon being able to step out of myself as we do to be in different places at the same time. I later learned that the other Ancients did not know they could do this."

"So, you taught them a new trick?"

"Yeah, then they decided to keep it under cover so to speak so that not all with power learned the trick since it could be dangerous in the wrong hands. Likewise, we, you and I can experiment with multiple identities, but keep our success quiet except to those we trust."

"My curiosity is peaked." Lyamy stated. Without hesitation she stepped out of herself taking on the form of an elf that could easily have been a sister to Chareece. With a few minor mistakes.

Chareece started laughing. "You may want to study the form you are changing to a little more before changing. You captured a lot of my likeness." She pointed to the elf form Lyamy so the normal Lyamy could see what she was laughing at. Cat ears, a hint of cat eyes still and a tail gave away she was not a real elf.

Lyamy nodded with a smile. In her elf form she adjusted the mistakes with easy. "It proves we can do it. If we can take the form of other living beings, what about objects?" The elf Lyamy shifted again taking on the appearance of the dresser in Chareece's room. Then she shifted again and stepped back into herself.

"Changelings." Chareece said almost in a whisper. "We are

creatures of legend. Stories told to children of times long ago about mischievous creatures known as changelings."

"I have never heard of them." Lyamy looked with curiosity at Chareece. "But from the sound of the name and what I just did, I am guessing something to do with being able to change form."

"They were creatures that were said to do mischief by taking on the form of someone and pulling pranks and the next day the person who may have not even been in the same town would get blamed. Legends say that after a King claimed it was not him that started a war and blamed the changeling, he met with a horrible end. After that changelings were hunted supposedly until they were extinct."

"They would not be so easily found if they could vanish into a different form in a crowd."

"Indeed, some say the changelings were benign pranksters who simply vanished to a more secretive life." Chareece pointed to books on her shelf. "There were thousands slain according to the legends and it seemed to be mostly political enemies accused of being changelings."

"That sounds so civilized." Lyamy said sarcastically.

"The stories became legends and then changelings were thought to be no more than stories to teach children lessons. There are over a thousand stories each with some moral underlining." Chareece shifted into an old lady and back. "Now I wonder how many of them are really true."

"Perhaps we should study that more before sharing even with those we trust."

"That is a good point, Lyamy. We had best run to the matters at hand. I have already given you the layout of the land. I would suggest your companions remain here in the city until you return after the event. You can use your speed and meet with the leaders of both camps in less than a day and provide communication between them almost instantaneously."

"You mean split again so I am in both places?" It was no longer a burden for Lyamy to be in so many locations at the same time, but the original plan was for one of her to attend to the needs of the two locations.

"That is not what I had in mind. Terriala has several maidens who serve her by choice grooming the gardens around the shrine they built. One of them could serve as Priestess to Sein Estel. You can provide them with a link so that they can share thoughts they choose across the distance." Chareece paused ever so slightly. "It would not be a bad idea though for you to split and be in both camps."

"I see it too. The closer we get the more the time threads show. The greatest indications of after effects are on this continent and in the threads for your followers. There are things effected everywhere, even in places that do not appear to currently exist. For the most part I can see the weaving of the threads, but not the events themselves."

"In part that is because decisions we make will impact the outcome, so results are not more than shadows before we make those decisions." Chareece walked over to her dresser and pour two glasses from a decanter, handing one to Lyamy and taking a sip from her own glass. "You have looked back through time also. The time of legends was destroyed by the abuse of temporal magic and what we are seeing now is part of the consequences of that abuse."

"It serves as a good warning for us to be careful with how we use the power we have." Lyamy accepted the glass and tasted the liquid from within. It filled her with warmth and a sense of being filled with energy and power. The flavor was like a blending of sun ripened fruit.

"First time sipping the nectar of the Ancients." Chareece smiled. "Nothing else can compare."

*   *   *   *

*

"We have studied everything else in the chest." Felps was protesting. "They are all powerful relics, but we have gotten no closer to understanding the black orb. I feel the time is closing in and we have to activate the device. The power of the device itself is driving me to do this."

"If we do not let him, it may drive him insane." Francis acknowledged.

"Five more days." Perinella insisted. "If we cannot figure anything out in five more days he can take it to a remote location and activate it. Then we can only hope it does not impact the entire world. Let's finish eating and we can go back and spend a few more hours analyzing the rest of the relics before we turn in for the night."

Felps grumbled and continued devouring what was on his plate.

"The power that has touched him is changing Felps. He is eating ten times what he ate before and he had a big appetite to start with.”

“I can see that Francis. What does it mean though, he is not growing a belly, where is the food going?”

“The rain brings the harbinger of the awakening.” Felps made another random comment. Someone else on a different continent shared the random comment. Chelic was with Lyamy gathering herbs in the fields not far from the sanctuary when she made the same statement. She was known for random prophetic comments she did not remember ever since she was brought back from death by ShadowDancer. The important part being Lyamy heard the words.

“You are not making sense again, Felps.” Perinella started cleaning up the dishes they were done with, when one of their servants stepped in and insisted it was her responsibility.

“One way or another we have to get him out from under the influence of that artifact soon.”

Later in the night, Felps went to his door and touched the lock. It felt like a dream and he did not really know what he was doing. A ripple went out as a point in space was twisted in time and the lock clicked. He opened the door and stepped out into the hall. The door closed, time returned to normal and the lock was again secured. Using the same manipulation of time, he moved as one sleep walking through other locked doors and pulled the orb and pedestal from the chest.

“They do not want us close.” he said to himself in a voice that was not his own.

"We can teleport to a place away from everyone." He answered in his own voice.

"I will grant you more power and you will be free again when we are done. We are saving an entire race from destruction. We are doing a good thing." The strange voice spoke again from within him.

"It is important to save a race from extinction. I agree." Felps etched the air with the arcane gestures. "Here we go." The portal opened and he stepped through, stepping out onto a mountain slope. He did not know exactly where he was, but he knew it was in an unpopulated area of the Northern continent based on the documentation they had. His information was old but looking around he felt comfortable that it was correct. There were no signs of roads or buildings and he could not see or smell any indications of civilization.

He had to find an ideal place to activate the orb. There had to be a big enough valley or area, and he had to be able to find a precipice to work from where he could see what was happening. His was the hand that would save them from oblivion. He felt a heavy sadness that he could not save them all and yet he did not even know who he was saving.

"They are the Baratir." The strange voice from within told him. "They were an innocent race until the lords of magic pulled them into the games. Other races chose to war on their own, but not the Baratir. They are fierce and savage, but they did not choose the fate of the wars."

"There were other races?"

"We could not save them all alone. We chose to save the one."

"We?" Felps shook his head. "Do you mean you and I?"

"No. Although you too have chosen to help." The voice inside him showed approval in the statement. "We is a reference to ourselves that those who worship us understand. We are one."

"You are like the Ancients of this world." Felps replied. "You are like gods, are you one of the lords of magic?"

"We are." The voice responded. "Your Ancients do not know the meaning of Ancient. We were before we can remember. Perhaps they are powerful enough to help me preserve what was, if any are willing."

"I do not know the Ancients, just know of them."

"That you are not at constant war tells me they are not as evil as the lords of magic were."

"Are you evil?"

"We are not evil. We are a part of a faction that turned against the evil, the never-ending war and killing. We used time manipulation to try and save a few here and there. We were accused of cheating, but then they all started manipulating time, each in more powerful ways. No care or understanding of what they did. They were sloppy and caused a cascading collapse in the flow of time, a chain reaction that destroyed the world we knew."

"You escaped the collapse?"

"Not completely, but I will return when you activate this orb. I must be there and gain strength to stand against the awakening."

"What awakening?"

"The magic lords who found ways to avoid getting lost in the end of the collapse. These Ancients of your, perhaps they will protect their world from the past. I must give them warning."

Felps continued climbing up and down seeking the ideal place for activation of the dark orb. He did not notice the passage of day or night as he walked around talking with the voice inside him.

*   *   *   *

*

There are events that time does not care about. Changing a series of events in time that change an entire civilization may go without concern. Changing a time known event so a new kingdom is formed or a kingdom that was supposed to be never existed can be done as long as you do not break a fixed event. Time has a way of correcting or adjusting events, flexible to the general flow.

There are fixed events in time that should not be tampered with or the consequences can be harsh no matter how innocent the intent. Time will rip apart surrounding events to correct the breaking of a fixed event. It is not what we see or perceive about the event that makes it fixed. If you change what hour in the day the sun comes up, it is not a big deal, but if you remove the hour of sunrise you break time. If you remove that placing of every twelfth rivet in a bridge, the bridge can collapse and may require rebuilding from scratch.

Fixed time events are not always obvious, but to know what about the event is fixed is the most important detail to consider before making any change. Time has a life of its own. If you break the hidden secrets that hold it together it will pull upon the fibers that make it up and rebuild the gap without concern for the consequences it does not see.

Many of the Ancients heard the scream or felt the ripple. Most assumed it was part of the coming time collision, just more of the raining effects. It was too close for HonorLord and Darvarias to ignore as they headed towards the farmhouse community. Lyamy recognized the voice and projected a copy of herself directly to the location.

Lyamy could see the frenzy of activity in the weaving of the threads of time. Altering looping stitching events together in a madness to fix a breach that was only just starting to be pulled back together. She could see the timelings creatures created by time itself for protection. She knew Grandma was gone, as if she had never existed. There were other cascading events that time was pulling back under control.

"You did this." a large timeling stopped and faced her. "It was a fixed event, why would you change a fixed event?"

"Compassion, I thought I had all the chain of events covered." She apologized.

The timeling changed its glare, to a slightly less harsh appearance. "I cannot stop you from making changes, you have the power. I can request before you touch another fixed event you call me." The creature handed her, a small black stone. "I can help you not collapse existence."

"Thank you. I will remember. I promise to consult you before I touch another fixed event." The timeling scuttled back to his business.

"Who are you talking to?" she recognized the voice of Darvarias even if she had not felt their arrival.

"The timeling." Lyamy shuddered suddenly as she felt something dark nearby. It felt like a dark shadow of herself.

"I don't see anything." Darvarias stated.

"She has the ability to see time." HonorLord stated as if it explained everything.

"People are gone because I made a mistake and altered a fixed point in time." she looked at the unexplainable loose ends that composed the events of the town. "They do not even know what they are missing. She has been removed, but not all the consequences of her actions. It was not her life that even mattered to time. I must die yet again to fix my blunder." She felt it again, it was her, but it was not her. It was very close.

"What are you talking about?" HonorLord looked confused

"The timeling will know. I must give this body up to fill the gap I left in the structure of time, to restore the fixed point." She turned quickly as she spoke. "I must die again, but not by your hand." As she caught the dagger wielding hand of the death changeling, she knew instantly what it was. It screamed in rage and flew back. Landing on the ground facing her. "You are bound. I order you to never do anything that will bring harm to me or my friends."

The creature looked like her only dark and angry. Cadabriana put her dagger in her belt and hissed in rage. "As you command. I was not expecting you here or I would have planned better. I could not resist such delightful anguish. They hurt and do not know why.”

Lyamy walked to wards the timelings the others could not see, “I offer a part of myself to close the breach and restore a new fixed point.”

The timelings stopped and turned to her. “Quickly then, make of yourself the time matter so we can rebuild the rend. If we can, we will restore the grandmother also.”

To the others watching she appeared to start disintegrating. The death changeling fed on the pain of the transition smiling knowing that Lyamy knew what she was but let her feed anyway. “She dies, and suffers, but is not dead.”

“What are you fowl creature?” Darvarias asked

“It does not matter; she will tell you now anyway. I am a Death Changeling from the time of legends. I was awakened by her last death.” Cadabriana stated gesturing in the direction that Lyamy had been.

“Time is shifting again.” HonorLord pointed to buildings that had vanished and now returned. “We had best avoid encountering anyone.”

“There suffering is gone.” Cadabriana was obviously disappointed.

HonorLord waved his hand and moved the people in front of them thirty feet to his right only a fraction of a second before a giant stone foot appeared partially integrated with whatever was left where it appeared. Where it overlapped with the buildings the structure ran into the stonework. A tree appeared to be growing through the big toes and sandal. The statue was broken off above the ankle about twenty-five feet from the ground.

"The rain from the time event?" Darvarias looked at HonorLord questioningly.

"Yes. We have the ability to do anything that the other Ancients can do." HonorLord pointed to the people. "I sensed the event coming. We may just have to work on developing the same sight and senses that they have innately. Just like they could have the same sense of war and battle as we do, but it comes naturally to us to know and they would have to develop the skill."

Darvarias nodded, "Like artists, some have the skill to paint or draw from birth, others can train and paint and draw although perhaps not as well as those who do so by nature?"

"Well put. We better return to what we were doing." The two of them vanished.

Cadabriana was disappointed that she made no great impact on these beings of power. They seemed to have more control than the old magic lords. She turned back towards Erhbron. Lyamy knew who she was there was no longer a need to hide. It would take her time to learn what her new master would allow her to get away with, what were her new limits. She failed to kill Lyamy before she was discovered. A few millennia of sleep can make one a little sloppy. For now, she did not have to stir the pot, she could live off the suffering that was already there.

*   *   *   *

*

Brent was delivering a wagon load of hides to the leather shop.

Rachel did not pay him the best prices, but she always paid him, and he liked her. She had given him a key to the back door so he could drop off the hides and he never took more than their agreed price from her till.

The shop was dark and quiet for the middle of the day as he stepped in and dropped the first stack of hides in the bin. It was too quiet, so he decided to look around. As he stepped from the supply room to the workshop behind the storefront, he saw her strapped to the wall. She was still alive, her eyes rolled in his direction.

There is a point where pain and fear succumb and lost their potency. From the look in her eyes, she had passed that point some time ago. Brent pulled his hunting knife and easily slit the leather straps holding her up on the wall. She was too parched to speak when he freed her from her bonds, and he had to hold her up and easy her to a seat. There was odd bruising under her skin. The summoned insects had returned to wherever they came from a few hours after they summoned so he did not know the cause.

He brought her water and helped her get comfortable. He would stay with her for a few days to nurse her back to health. He did not know then this would lead to a closer permanent relationship.

*   *   *   *

*

It was not a surprise this time, so she was braced for it through her multi-present state. Lyamy set down the glass and leaned on the dresser for a moment while she felt the dismembering of her body like a million bug bites at the same time. A tear formed in the corner of her eye. She picked the glass back up and drank the rest of the contents feeling the restorative power of the nectar and taking a deep breath.

Chareece felt the death and her eyes filled with anger, but Lyamy held up her hand. "A sacrifice I had to make to fix a mistake I made that broke a fixed point in time."

"You will have to share the story when we have time." Chareece calmed quickly. "We must make haste. The event is in motion."

Lyamy nodded. "On my way." She stepped out on Chareece's balcony and Pterdin appeared as she sent the thought. Lyamy climbed on his back and gave him the added speed she had with her caress on his neck as he lifted off. If someone happened to look up at best, they might have seen a golden streak across the sky. They moved fast enough it was difficult to make out any detail ahead of them before they passed it.

They were over the walls of the city in minutes and racing over the flat lands towards the mountains. She saw what she assumed was Lone Peak ahead and to their right. It was the largest known active volcano that stood alone near the edge of the mountain ranges. They were passing the volcano in less than an hour from the time they launched off the balcony, what would normally be a five-day journey.

Pterdin took them straight east over the mountains. The air was thin and cold. Lyamy generated a field to protect them from the cold. They could deal with the thin air for a while. The mountains were covered in ice and snow as they flew over, an occasional outcropping of rock

214

peeking out from under the white blanketing. Lyamy found the view in the late afternoon light to be quite breathtaking the cast of light and shadow sprinkled with a sparkling of flashing color from the prismatic effects of the ice.

At lower levels the trees gave texture to the slopes and even lower the denser forest gave a darker texture with an appearance of a sprinkling of white powder. She decided as she flew that she would take the time to fly all around the world to see the panorama of the different lands. If she could capture the awe and thrill of seeing this for the first time and share that with others, like Freyie from her den back home.

It felt like she had always known Freyie. They were cubs together, then blood rivals when they became apprentices. She became Lyamy's best friend after Lyamy spared her life with a price when Freyie had slipped into her room. The price was Freyie was bound to Lyamy and subject to anything Lyamy willed her to do. The bond was later eased with the help of ShadowDancer, but Freyie remained as Lyamy's best friend. She would have to take her to the skies and give her a chance to see the wondrous view.

Lost in thought and distracted by the view, Pterdin was descending before Lyamy realized they had reached the Tent City and Shrine to ShadowDancer. There was activity in the clearing where they landed and Pterdin vanished as she dismounted although she could still feel his presence. She had gotten used to knowing he was there. She did not have to adjust to having land legs, being multi-present gave her the resources of her other selves to immediate access of ability.

Those in the clearing had moved back as the dragon had landed, but now that Pterdin had vanished they were more comfortable at approach her. The larger number stopped at a respectable distance and a man she would read as being half human and half elf stepped forward hand extended.

"Greetings, I am Samuel. We have been expecting you. Please follow me to Terriala."

Lyamy shook his hand, "I am Lyamy avatar of ShadowDancer. It is a pleasure to meet you Samuel." He turned and lead the way along a path that was worn clear by use. They entered a small clearing completely covered by the canopy of the forest. In the middle of the clearing stood a statue, bigger than life, of ShadowDancer that Lyamy had seen before only in a dream.

Terriala seated in front of the statue on a pad on the ground opened her eyes and looked up at Lyamy. Lyamy pulled back her hood and Terriala quickly rose to her feet. "It is a pleasure and an honor to meet you Lyamy. I am Terriala and my sister has spoken highly of you." Terriala bowed slightly acknowledging Lyamy.

Lyamy returned the gesture of respect. "Terriala, High priestess of ShadowDancer, it is my honor and pleasure to meet you. You are aware of why I am here." Lyamy looked around the clearing and at the entrance to the cave. "You have done very nice work here."

"Yes, I know why you are here. Cellina has showed her dedication from the beginning and would serve well as a priestess to Sein Estel." Terriala gestured to a young woman who was nurturing the vine walls that formed an enclosure around the clearing. Cellina turn and offered a gracious curtsy to Lyamy. She appears to be part elf, but her skin had a slight green hue her small elegant tusks suggested why she may have been considered an outcast. "You are also here to help with our defense meaning the big event is close at hand."

"Are you ready to make the journey, Cellina." Lyamy stepped out of herself in her direction.

"I am." She took Lyamy's outstretched hand and the two of them vanished in a blur of speed.

"My I look inside your cave." the Lyamy that remained in front of Terriala asked.

"Of course." Terriala smiled and lead the way through the concealing vines and down the twelve steps to the large metal chamber. "I can see thoughts Cellina is sharing."

Lyamy looked it over, quite capable of holding a few hundred soldiers if necessary. "You are the high priestess, and she is one of your priestesses. This way you can share knowledge immediately."

"Only what we willingly share though." Terriala examined this new ability with Cellina.

Lyamy turned to the left and then left again so she was facing the wall next to the entrance. She placed her hands on the wall and a depression formed in the wall with another statue. It was the perfect likeness of Terriala life size on a small pedestal. Engraved on the pedestal were the words: *"Terriala First High Priestess to ShadowDancer"*. Lyamy drew a piece of Terriala's spirit out and placed it in the statue. "You are immortalized."

"You put a part of me into that statue? I felt you draw from my essence." Terriala looked a bit confused.

"I did indeed. I have learned not to break fixed points in time, so I will work around them. Prick your finger and put three drops in the chalice your statue is holding."

Terriala was obviously uncertain about what she was doing but did as Lyamy requested. For a moment when the third droplet landed Terriala was looking out of the eyes of the statue. Then though shaken a bit she was back holding her hand over the chalice. "What did you do to me?"

"This statue is a resurrection stone." Lyamy placed her hand on the statue and it glowed with a divine aura and faded. "I know and ShadowDancer will know. This stone will not work if you choose not to return when the time comes. You cannot be forced to return."

"You know when I will die." Terriala touched the statue with an odd respect.

"Do not worry, it is not until well after the events we are currently preparing for and no I will not tell you nor speak of it again."

"You have a full copy of me in that statue. Something like the way you step out of yourself. If I learn I can look through the eyes of the statue, I can feel it."

"Do not put yourself into the statue, be careful. I will teach you if you want to learn." we have a little time while we wait. Tomorrow we will head north into the mountains with a very small group."

*   *   *   *

*

Lyamy took Cellina by the hand and accelerated her. Within a few steps nobody else could see anything more than the blur they left behind. She did not have to hurry. Lyamy touched Terriala and built the bond between her and Cellina before turning and leaving the clearing. With each step they leaped a portion of the distance closer to Sein Estel.

"We share thoughts now." Cellina observed out loud. "I mean Terriala and I. It is like we can talk with just our minds to each other."

"It is to help you be an effective priestess."

"I did not know what to expect when she pulled me to the side and told me I would be the priestess to Sein Estel. She showed me how to bless weapons and we went over everything she could think of that might help."

"You are not all elf, but you are more than half elf." Lyamy invited more information with her manner.

"A creature appeared out of nowhere when my mother was young. It was lost, something like these events that have been happening more recently. The ground at the creature's feet was different from the land around it. It was injured and my grandmother nursed it back to health. My mother was born from that nursing. She was fortunate enough to find a good elf who found love for her." Cellina stopped as if that explained everything.

"Next step Sein Estel." When they reached the town Lyamy paused turning to Cellina. "You need to be dressed in the proper attire as priestess." Cellina's clothing changed to match those of Terriala, black and gold in a pattern emulating flames, scant but concealing. It had the same characteristics ShadowDancer had given the outfit for her high priestess. The outfit would provide protection from weather conditions and defend her as if she were wearing armor. Along with the outfit a staff appeared in her hand topped with a flame of shadow and fire that would not go out.

They did a quick tour of the town getting the general layout before Lyamy changed her appearance to that of the avatar wearing only flame and shadow and slowed them down to a speed that others could see. They appeared just inside the doorway of the town meeting hall. Delmar and Peltricia were seated with a few of the town's council members. "Greetings, elders of Sein Estel."

They looked up slightly startled by their quiet arrival. They all stood up with brief whispering as to who the strangers were at the door. "Welcome, please come in." Delmar waved them towards the front of the room where they had been seated. "By your appearance I would guess you are Lyamy avatar of ShadowDancer and you are the priestess sent to give us guidance when we need it."

"We were informed you would be arriving before some big event happens that may impact us. Please allow us to extend our hospitality and that of the town while we have time. I am Peltricia, this is Delmar and members of the Sein Estel council." Peltricia gave a bow of her head and a slight curtsy.

"We accept your hospitality. This is Cellina, she shall serve as your priestess. I am sure you have temporary housing to accommodate her needs until something permanent is established. If you can I would like a space where you can find me while I am here." Just as Lyamy finished speaking a "raindrop" fell. I tree appeared in the middle of the meeting hall that looked as though it belonged in a tropical climate with large frond leaves and a sectional trunk of a monocotyledon structure. With a gesture, Lyamy sent it to the island where she had been sending other things, not far from her home at the sanctuary on the savage continent. "We do not have long, but these events are going to become very intense. You need patrols watching for living creatures coming through and watch for incidents that may get any of our people caught in the event."

The others watch silently for a few moments while Lyamy rebuilt the structure of the building that had been supplanted by the time event. Peltricia broke out of the state of awe first. "Do we know what to expect from this time collision?"

"Wherever it happens, there is going to be a major area impacted. If anyone happens to be in the impacted area, they may experience dire consequences. What would have happened if someone was sitting where that tree just appeared? Some of these smaller events we have seen displace what is there, moving it, some have replaced what was there like this tree did, perhaps pushing what was here before out of place in time, others seem to merge with what is there already. We have not witnessed every event, so we are still not sure what to expect."

"So, we can expect an increase in these events at an accelerated rate just before the big event, but we do not know when or what is happening." Delmar was obviously frustrated as he turned towards the door. "I will set up all our patrols and put them on watch for anything that may pose a threat. Oh, and Cellina, you can pick from any of the spare houses we built on the western side of town against the mountains. We will do any customizing you want."

"He does not like, not knowing what he is dealing with, but he will give marked detail to ensuring the safety of our people." Peltricia smirked after Delmar as he went out the door. "You wanted space; I take it you do not mean a room where you can sleep. There are some smaller rooms here in this building we use for small meetings or doing paperwork and things like that if you want to use one of them."

"The smallest room would be great. If you cannot find me, just knock on the door and call, I will answer." Lyamy did not need space really, just a door. She could make whatever space she needed. The real purpose was so if she was off patrolling herself and they needed her they could call her. To them she was still the avatar to ShadowDancer, it was not time to tell them she had been elevated to the status of an Ancient.

"I will return and stay here after I select a house." Cellina stated. "I can bless weapons for defending and provide direct communication with the shrine camp, Samuel and Terriala."

Peltricia gave an elegant curtsy. "I am going to see to arrangements for a feast in honor of your presence Avatar Lyamy and your arrival Priestess Cellina. What is ours is yours." The other council members left with her.

Lyamy nodded to Cellina and she departed also to pick her house. Lyamy tuned to the door she had picked. The room behind it was a little bigger than a closet, but she opened a dimensional space and placed windows along the walls similar to those she had seen when she visited ShadowDancer. The windows provided a view that scanned the landscape between Sein Estel and the shrine camp. Praka was not far east from the area in between, but from what she could see of the time threads the township of Praka was no in immediate danger.

*   *   *   *

*

The valley was good. It was wide and open in the middle of nowhere. The voice told him it was big enough. He was high enough up overlooking the valley to be safe from harm's way. Carefully he placed the orb and pedestal on the edge of the ledge. The voice had been teaching him the ritual as they traveled. He etched the symbols in the ground. He built the symbols of wood and stone and placed the pot of water over a fire in the middle. He stood a wood staff in the ground with a string of feathers on a braided thread hanging from the top immediately catching the wind.

When everything was ready and in place, he sat down facing the orb pressed against the base of the golden podium that held it and a small chamber opened that could not previously be seen. Pressing his finger against the small spine that stuck up in the bottom of the indent it only took a few drops of blood to fill the hollow. He called upon the elemental forces and the primordial powers. He sat with his eyes closed so there was no one to see the display of power form the elemental and primordial realms. Then he called upon time itself to return that which had been pulled out of place.

Felps slipped into a trance. History sped before his eyes as he plunged into the past. Felps found himself in a round room on the opposite side of a magic circle from a sorcerer of at least twice his stature. He looked up at the man in blue robes and a billowing thick white beard, so think it looked more like a rich man's pillow stuffing then a beard. His robes were made of a very thick material, blue with stars and spheres moving across the surface of the material. His robes had a high cowl pulled back so as not to hide his face and a wide brimmed cloth hat folded over on the top. In his left hand was a staff tipped with a sphere and smaller spheres moving in every direction in circles around it but never colliding.

Felps looked at the floor and the patterns on the floor were complex with circles and lines that moved while held in stone and metal. He knew that the symbolism although he had never before seen it had to do with time. He recognized that some of what he saw was writing in a language unknown. The right hand of this sorcerer was holding him here

224

in time and it was clear there was a great strain in doing so. "I am Felps Delucette. I am guessing you know I am from the future, since I think you brought me here. Actually, I am just guessing that too."

"I am Time Wizard Luumeheru. Yes, I have brought you back through time although just your conscience. I am calling upon you to spare an innocent race from the destruction brought on to this world by the Wizards of Time. We have collectively sent this world and who knows what else into a cascading collapse of time. Recovery will take millennium."

"You are straining, tell me quickly what you need me to do." Felps recognized Luumeheru as the voice that was inside him.

"You Felps are fea lipsa my cleansing spirit from the future that will help me with one small deed to atone for a tiny piece of my involvement in the end of our time, no matter how small. I need to share with your enough for you to choose to assist me although I appreciate your open trust, never make a time decision without knowing the details."

"If I don't help you, you will find someone else who will. And if the decision was not already made, I would not have had the key and destiny to go as far as I have."

"This is true, but you still must make the decision. As I explain events to you, you will see them in a vision to help you understand." The air sizzled in the circle between them, and a sphere opened and Luumeheru told his story of the events and the escalation of the wars, wrapped in an effort to avert the destruction they were creating. Felps lost track of time, but knew that somehow, he would remember every detail when things were done. He learned the language of the Time Wizards, both spoken and written. It felt like months had passed before they were done. He was confident when they were done that, he was in fact doing the right thing and not just because he trusted Luumeheru.

He returned to himself with confidence he was doing the right thing. The feeling he may be losing his mind and the idea that the voice was delusional faded away. The predawn light was beginning to illuminate the sky when he started uttering the words. The random events were changing the appearance of the mountains around the valley, preceding the completion of the invocation. Time rippled harder and faster. A rip opened spreading wide in the valley below him. He spoke the final words "sanga heru luu o pel" The language of the elves was around long before the elves themselves, although the original writing would not have been recognized.

*   *   *   *

*

The rate of events had increased through the night even within the limits of Sein Estel creature appeared and ran, while objects materialized in places they should not be. The people of the town were getting familiar enough to be able to avoid being in a location where an event was about to happen. Among other things a soldier of an unknown race appeared injured outside in front of the meeting hall. Cellina pushed the folks gathered around aside as she walked up but was not prepared for what she saw. The man fit the description of her grandfather. His skin was green multiple short tusks up and down pointed ears. There were hints of scales in protective areas of his skin.

He uttered words in an unknown language and showed some relief when he saw Cellina's face. A flash of frustration showed on his face when she did not understand him. She placed her hand upon his wounds and began pushing healing into his being. His injuries were deep and without her divine healing he would surely have died before they could carry him into a building. "Bring water and food." she ordered as one of authority and others did as she instructed. "Bring a tarp and blankets and carry him in to a table in the meeting hall."

He was obviously a warrior but stripped of weapons. She pulled his armor off with care and ministered to his wounds as she found them. When she was done, he was stripped completely and covered with a blanket sleeping with only the padding of the tarp and blanket under him on the firm wooden table. She sent his clothing and armor to be cleaned and repaired and asked for additional clothing he could wear while that was being done.

Other townsfolk brought in five others one of them was same race and four of them from different race into the hall for her care. The last one did not survive; her injuries were too severe. They all appeared to have been pulled from the middle of a battle. Reports indicated that several had appeared that still had the strength and ability to flee into the forest. One of the townsfolk came in holding an injured arm about the time the early glow of morning first started to show. He had been struck by a soldier who appeared and then ran off when he realized it was not his enemy. Lyamy was attending to this would when the ripple and rumble began.

The shaking of the ground was not hard, but it was long and combined with the rippling of time. The dis-joining and reuniting of movement and time had a nauseating effect. Lyamy could see timelings everywhere working intelligently to keep the thread of time from shattering under the pressure. It was as if time was trying to rip itself apart, or perhaps pulling itself back together after a long lost absence.

*   *   *   *

*

The tent city at the Shrine Camp was inundated with an increase of fallout from the time events. Samuel and Terriala kept things organized as the flurry of activity kept everyone from sleeping. A seventy-foot statue appeared in the middle of camp and fell over breaking to pieces and tearing a rip in the forest because the ground was not solid enough to support the weight. A giant winged creature appeared and took to the air dropping feathers and scales bigger than the people as it vanished.

Random soldiers of four different races appeared some injured, some still swinging their weapons. They stopped fighting when they realized they were not in the middle of their war. They could not communicate until one of the injured wearing a robe spoke in a language that was very much like elvish. When they answered in elvish the creature seemed a little surprised stating "You speak the language of the time wizards."

He did not understand the word for elf, but he understood that there was a different reference for the language then he was familiar with otherwise the language was close enough to communicate. In turn he knew the languages of the other races. The result was he became the translator, and they were limited in how many of the others they could speak with at a time.

It took time to start piecing together the bits of what was happening where they came from. They were at war, some of them were even enemy soldiers. They were under the command and control of different time wizards, serving because they had to. Once away and out from under their control they had no more reason to fight each other. They refused to say anything bad about the Time Wizards just in case they were listening. It seemed as if these time wizards may have been a lot like the Ancients before they changed their ways.

The ancients used to breed races and use their powers to play games building and warring races against each other for entertainment. Some of the Ancients lead by Gaharias recognized at some point that the races they were toying with had the potential to evolve and grow into the power they had. They started realizing the people were more than just game pieces, they had a consciousness and an awareness making them less like game pieces on a board and more like children to be cared for and nurtured. Lyamy concluded that the Time Wizards caused their own destruction before they woke up to see what they were doing.

The predawn glow lit the sky. Nobody had enough sleep after

an entire night of chaos. Lyamy saw the ripple coming and then the time wavering had an effect on everyone. Objects became out of synchronization in time falling through tables, getting displaced. Some objects were displaced and resynchronized overlapping other objects, a plate and a cup overlapped and became one object, a bush became part of a tree. Lyamy saw the timelings although nobody else seemed to know they were there.

The timelings rush about, correcting some shifts, leaving others, but diligent about mending and pulling back to general order the threads of time. Lyamy noticed that the timelings were keeping any of the people from getting merged with other things, including each other.

The rumbling of the ground was felt and heard immediately after the time ripples. The time ripples and the rumbling did not seem to have a focus point of origin, but rather just happening everywhere at once. Then as mysteriously as the event began there was silence. The ripple had reached well beyond the planetary system they were in. Lyamy could not see the limit of the scope. She knew the event had happened and it was time to deal with the consequences and the rain of mini-events that would follow.

There was a central focus to the event even if the ripples and rubles did not radiate from that location, the intensity of related events tapered off with distance from that point. It was in the mountains to the north of the tent city and shrine camp. Like throwing a ball of mud there were splatter effects also. The magic or power used to do this was handled without

230

precise control. It bothered Lyamy that such great power could be wielded in such a sloppy manner.

Growing up in her clan life had been hard and to be sloppy meant death. The clan used the primordial magic and even though they practice through ritual and primitive methods, they had to be precise and use the power they had in an articulate fashion. The she grew and learned, the more power she was given the more control and discipline was required to be effective. The discipline of physical combat training overflowed in her life to her magical skills, if you kick at empty air it leaves you vulnerable. Vulnerability means weakness and weakness means death.

Lyamy could feel the army moving south, they were coming straight for tent city. War crazed confused and lost an army yanked out of time. They have been dropped in a strange world with a battle mob mentality. She had to stop them before there was conflict. She turned and was not really surprised to see HonorLord, the ancient of war appear next to her. ShadowDancer also arrived as quickly as she shared her thoughts.

*   *   *   *

*

The last far-reaching event that shook the world of Ethar was when the world cracked. Dead rose and the anger of a goddess was awakened. The collision of time enveloped the world in a time ripple, a rumble and shake felt in every corner and to the core of the planet, perhaps even reaching to the corners of space. It was a shake and rumble that could wake things long asleep that would be best left sleeping. How many were stirred from slumber, how many survived, and how many would survive waking up were questions nobody knew to ask. Nobody living knew the lords from the times of legends would ever return. They destroyed Ethar once before and if anyone living knew they would have done everything they could to prevent their return.

Oondoheru knew before the end those who slept, and he did everything he could to give the world time to recover and perhaps grow strong enough to ward off the lords of destruction. He could not undo the work of Luumeheru, but he could force it to take time. He pulled his work deep into the heart of the world buried in stone. Oondoheru placed protections and alarms around the chamber. The fact he was awake now meant those measures had finally failed. The stone around him turned to liquid and as he opened the way to where the chamber should have been, instead of deep rock he faced an open ocean.

Time moves all things. The depths are brought to the surface and mountains are pulled to the depths. The world reshapes itself into something new and hides what is old. Luumeheru had no way of knowing his work to save one race would lead to the other lords escaping their destruction and using it to sleep until the world was rebuilt. Oondoheru would stand with him if they could find each other. Luumeheru had not slept, he took a different path, but the awakening meant he also should have returned.

They were not the only two who had risen above the basic drives that might makes right and frowned upon the simplistic thinking of the other wizard lords. Their failure to think beyond the next victory kept them forever at work and lead to the destruction of all they knew. It was not until the end was in sight that they even began to think about a future. They used the work of Luumeheru to to link their own hibernation. The collision it would cause was set as an alarm to trigger their awakening.

Stone shifted at his will, providing him a path across the ocean that vanished behind him. Oondoheru had to warn him, Luumeheru, and join forces and protect this new world from the awakening of the other wizard lords. He could feel his presence to the north. Oondoheru could feel the others waking up.

*   *   *   *

*

The rumbling stopped and Felps opened his eyes. In front of him instead of the orb and pedestal stood a person of sorts. Very large and wearing the robes he saw in his vision. As the giant three times his height turned around, he already knew it was Luumeheru. "We have succeeded for now, Felps. We have brought them through time and the Baratir may have a chance of surviving beyond the destruction of my time."

Looking at the flat body of land that filled the valley and was covered in soldiers to far away for details Felps spoke with hesitation. "They are an army, an army that is war crazed and they are moving as if chasing an enemy that is not here. We must bring them to reason."

"They will come around after they have run off their battle rage. You have gained some knowledge of the language and learning of my time. I promised you reward and I will deliver.”

"This place is somewhat remote, up here in the mountains, but if they rampage, they could be upon an innocent town in very little time.” Felps was in a state of alarm. “We brought them through for their survival, not to make new enemies in a new time. “Reward can wait we have lives to protect.”

Luumeheru was surprised at Felps’ concern for the wellbeing of others he did not know over his own reward. For the first time he realized the help provided was more out of compassion for the salvation of the Baratir then it was for the reward. “Felps, your compassion is refreshing. We must do what we can, but I will grant you part of your reward immediately, since it will help in the effort.” A pulse from the staff Luumeheru was holding hit Felps. “You will now understand the languages of my time written and spoken.”

The Baratir had vanished from the new plateau in what was previously a valley heading south across the mountains. “Thank you, but we need to move.” Luumeheru was obviously willing because when Felps touched him and stepped using his mage step spell they both went to the edge of the woods where the Baratir had disappeared. “Can you sense where they are? I have to admit I am not yet a master of magic, I just know a calamity of various spells. We can probably catch up and communicate with them faster using your power.”

“Your use of power is much cleaner, more crisp results, perhaps when we are done, we can share knowledge.” Luumeheru noted that there were no extemporaneous materials that traveled with them. "I can take us to the trailing forces, and we can start by explaining to them then leap to the next until we have called them all to gather. They are not my followers, so I do not have a way to address them all at once."

"Let's go then." Felps was anxious. He did not want to be responsible for causing a disaster or massacre. "We need to stop them before they get too far."

"They have no reason to trust us or know who we are. They can as easily attack us when we stop them." Luumeheru said as hit etched the ritual symbols in the air and they teleported along with bits of the ground and pieces of the bushes that were around them.

Felps found himself appearing within feet of the Baratir moving away from them. "Stop." he called in their language. "Your war is long over." He cast a web spell that brought a group about forty feet ahead to a stop and those behind them after some confusion.

Those that had been brought to a stop turned around on their assailants. Weapons at the ready that started towards the two wizards. Luumeheru gestured and a blue barrier appeared. The Baratir soldiers stopped and dropped to one knee at the appearance of the barrier. Luumeheru bellowed, "You have been pulled from battle to a safe haven. Any in these lands are innocent to our wars. We need to stop fighting."

"What should we do, wizard lords?" One member of the group asked.

"Return to the clearing you just came from so we can organize what happens once we have everyone back." Luumeheru instructed. "We must continue to inform the rest. There is no reason for your people to die or kill other innocent people any longer."

They proceeded from group to group doing the same thing. Felps had a ton of questions but refrained from asking and focused on the more urgent matter of convincing as much of this army to stop and back off as they could before it was too late. The army was moving quickly and Felps was certain they would come well short of stopping them all. Felps wished humans had access to the Ancients, he would call on them now if they did.

*   *   *   *

*

Eric was the most powerful of all Ancients, although he had less experience and less time spent in the universe than most. His lust had always been for knowledge not power. Many years ago, now he received power and was granted access to limitless knowledge. He was a hero on Ethar but maintained a low profile with his double life on earth. He had been asked to track all the fallout he could from the time collision event outside of Ethar.

At first, he caught random scattered bit that were appearing in time flux, placing them on a secluded island on Ethar. The frequency and number of life forms increased so he made a new dimensional plain and a world where he could start transferring everything that came through. He started by taking everything back from the secluded island and placing it in his new world, then pulled everything he saw come through outside of

Ethar through to this new world.

The further out he reached the more time debris he seemed to find. This time event had effects reaching more than just Ethar, but he still pulled everything that came through back to his newly created world. The closer the key event came the more scattered events came through the more life and the more sentient life came through. He could feel that some of the more sentient beings that came through were in a sleep state, but emanated power. He placed everything on the surface of the new world.

In all he salvaged seven wizard lords from the depths of space. Their protective measure to shield themselves from the time event failed. Eric was gaining knowledge with each event he touched and knew that the warring of these wizard lords was the cause of the catastrophic event that destroyed the life of the world at the end of the time of legends. He also knew that they were all riding the trailing of one known as the time wizard in hopes of surviving to a new day.

Those he rescued from space were not a part of the order of events for Ethar. Nothing came through that would be more then space debris. Nothing came through in space big enough to have an impact on events or register as a fixed point in time.

Eric was amused when he thought about their abilities to see time. Here he and ShadowDancer have had this power all along and it took Lyamy an avatar adopted by ShadowDancer to open their eyes to what they had. It was humbling, a reminder of where he came from, once a normal mortal himself and refreshing to see new blood spurn new thinking.

There was a great rush when the collision took place. Eric was sure he rescued at least a fourth of the lost world from space to the new world he had created. He could also see the whip tail through time of events, mini time collisions that would reach into the distant future. He would not pull the events that took place on Ethar to his alternative world, that would be a changing of the course of history and the order of the time lines. Time knew when it was ripped apart and began the repairing an correcting of course back then. Time knew and prepared for the collision of the past with the future. There was no need for him to start pulling at those threads.

*   *   *   *

*

Lyamy, ShadowDancer and HonorLord stood at the lead of the defensive line. They could feel the approaching army. It was diminishing in sized as portions seemed to be picked away from the rear forces and turned back. "We do not want to kill them, but we do not want them killing my followers either." ShadowDancer stated.

"This is not an outside influence event to Ethar. I can act as I am a part of Ethar, but I cannot implement anything that will cause a major change in the future history outside of my role as Ancient of war and High Lord of ShadowKeep." HonorLord stated.

"I have no restrictions." Lyamy stated and, "I will do whatever I can. I can disarm them and do things to stop their forward movement. Without their knowledge of what is happening."

238

"We do not need to do that. We can put up a barrier and protect our people from any attack long enough to possibly reason with them and give them time for their battle rage to cool down."

The lead edge of the army came close enough to see and the air filled with arrows and projectiles. In an instant ShadowDancer had the blue barrier field up and the projectiles all hit and slid to the ground. The next wave of projectiles was much smaller, but they appeared inside the shield instead of passing through it. Lyamy disappeared into a blur and most of these projectiles were ripped out of the air before they actually hit anything.

Rends started appearing in the barrier as some magic was being cast on the other side. ShadowDancer was able to refill the holes before the wave of projectiles reached the barrier. This army was familiar with fighting against pretty powerful magics. HonorLord pointed to the barrier and the color started shifting, but the holes stopped forming. The barrier would hold without their attention for hours now.

The army on the other side of the barrier dropped to all fours and suddenly the ground started shaking in waves, knocking those inside the encampment off their feet. ShadowDancer yelled in her native tongue, elvish, "Enough!!" and time stopped. She stepped through the barrier with Lyamy and HonorLord.

The three of them spread out. They targeted those that looked like leaders. Lyamy noted that a lot of their armor consisted of animal hides and the skin color beneath the armor was random multicolor. These were the creatures she saw in her visions of the future that came from the past. She grabbed one of the leaders looking ones and pulled him into the moment. He started to swing at her but stopped seeing all his comrades frozen in place.

"You spare us when you could destroy us." the soldier observed. "What has happened, we are not in the land where we were supposed to be fighting, but our orders were to kill all in our path?"

"You have been pulled out of time. Those who gave you orders are no longer here and the enemy you fought is also gone. You have no fight with these people, and we have no desire to kill you. If you do not stop the attack though, we will have no other choice."

"Speak with those wearing the orange armbands. I command twenty, the blue armbands command one hundred, but orange one thousand." She noted that his armband was red. Without hesitation she moved to the nearest orange banded soldier. As she stepped away from the first, he was frozen back in time.

The first orange armband soldier was a little more arrogant. "Who are you that you dare face me alone?" He swung his battle club at her, but she moved too fast. Disarming him in the blur of speed laying his club at his feet.

"I am Lyamy and it is time to stop this fight. You would much rather be forging metal frames and wheels for farming equipment. You have no fight with these people and those who pulled you from your life to fight are no longer. We would prefer not to have to kill you."

240

He swung his fist at her, and she landed him on his back with little effort. "You are serious, you do not wish to kill us. Do you plan on making us slaves?" He spun around attempting to sweep her feet out from under her.

She sidestepped his sweep, picked up his club and planted it handle down in the ground between his legs. "I have no use for slaves and no desire to put anyone else in bondage unless they force my hand."

"Perhaps you cannot kill. Then I have nothing to fear from you." He sat up not attacking her this time. "I am Breltak. Prove to me you can kill, and I will respect your request to stop battle."

Faster than he could see she had him back on his feet with a dead eliko, one of the local antelope at his feet and a heart in his hand. Time froze again for him as she moved on to the next. She was glad he was the only one that required she prove herself. She did not know he was the commander of the entire army.

When they were satisfied, they moved back behind the barrier and let go of the moment. Breltak the commander of the Baratir army watched the heart in his hand beat its last beat and barked out the commands. He held the heart up and then placed it upon the fallen beast. The fighting was over. He was no longer an enemy to the encampment and knew the ways of the magic. He walked through the barrier and straight up to Lyamy. "The day is yours." He said and offered her his club.

"The day is ours." She answered. "You have no enemy here, no surrender. Your weapon is yours."

HonorLord stepped up. "You have been honorable in battle. Your heart is pure. As Ancient of war, I grant you the power of the great bear."

Breltak looked at him with respect as he felt the surge of strength fill him. "You are not the wizard lords, but you have their power." He paused but a moment. "You have something more."

ShadowDancer spoke. "You were pulled from your lives to fight a war that was not yours. You were pulled from your world to a place and time you know nothing about. We must find for you a place you can call your own." She waved the barrier vanished.

"Where other than the forbidden continent will we find land that does not have some claim already placed upon it?" HonorLord asked. "As much as I am the Ancient of war, I have no desire to place anyone in a position that can create a grudge that leads to war."

"We can create one. We have more ocean than land. We can reshape an area to create a new landmass that can accommodate everything that has come from the time of legends."

"That would be a grand idea." Luumeheru said as he and Felps appeared next to them. The unasked request for help from Felps gave all three of them the knowledge of the situation they needed.

"Luumeheru, Felps, greetings." Lyamy greeted them by name. "You have brought no small stir to the world. Oondoheru is almost here to join you and help protect the world from the awakening that follows."

Luumeheru looked surprised. "You mean Oondoheru found a way to survive? And there are others?" His face was very serious. "This is

242

not good if the war I pulled these people from has followed me to a new epoch."

"Your power is chaotic and sloppy." ShadowDancer held no punches. "Are all of your," pausing looking for the word, "wizard lords as sloppy with the way they use magic?"

"We were born with power. Magic is not precise like the edge of a sword. What you wield with magic you cannot see. It does what you want, and there are other effects that are the price for using magic."

"You cannot see the magic you use?" Lyamy was surprised. There were no magic forces she used before she saw them.

"The rituals you did when you where clan would still have worked if you did not see the magic, Lyamy. They would have been sloppy like this, but they would have gotten the job done, you just would lack the precise control." ShadowDancer turned back to Luumeheru. "You cannot truly be a lord of the power you wield unless you can control it with precision."

The ground shook with the footsteps of something heavy approaching. "Oondoheru is here." Luumeheru stated. "I can feel his presence aside from his footsteps shaking everything."

"Luumeheru, we must prepare. Your own people betrayed you after you left in hopes of finding a way to spare themselves from the end. Word got out almost as soon as you left. Most of the other wizard lords managed to find a way to transcend the time. Your return will trigger the awakening of all." Oondoheru appeared not to see anyone else that was standing there with Luumeheru

"I am aware my friend. You must meet my friends here who think of our magic as sloppy." Luumeheru smiled gesturing in their direction.

Oondoheru looked down as if seeing them for the first time. "Sloppy?"

"Yes." Lyamy stepped up first. "If you want to cut down a tree you take out a swath of the forest, that is sloppy. I am Lyamy." She looked up at Oondoheru who stood about seventeen feet looming above her.

ShadowDancer stepped up before Oondoheru could start laughing. "She is right you are sloppy. You have power and knowledge of the others who will be waking up if they are not already awake. We can use your help in keeping things under control and perhaps if you are worthy, we can teach you to better control what you are doing."

Oondoheru did not conceal his anger. "We seek assistance in protecting your world, but if you think you and your LITTLE friends can be openly insolent to your betters who would stand in your defense you better be prepared to back up your words."

ShadowDancer saw the threads of power as Oondoheru began his casting and simply undid the weaving as fast as he performed his ritual, and nothing happened. "I see the threads of power you are trying to manipulate. You have the disadvantage. Size does not equate to power." She wove the threads he had been touching and bound his feet in stone without ritual. "You see, I do not need your ritual to weave the magic, I see the threads and weave them at will."

He lifted his foot and the stone shattered from his strength. "You have some power, I grant you, but it is feeble to hold me in place. Perhaps though you could help us."

"You have left your world and entered into our world, even if it is the same world at a different time. I do not need stone to hold you in place." ShadowDancer bound him in blue threads of the ancients magic he could not see. "This is our world, and we are the caretakers of the races. We will let you assist and be free in doing so, but you have to accept who is in charge. We have no desire to fight you as long as you do not wish to bring harm to our people, but we will not accept you stepping in and thinking you can have autonomous control of our world."

Oondoheru was unable to move or break the bonds that held him. "Perhaps I made an error in judgment. I concede to your power. Release me and I will assist you against the impending threat."

"You need to respect others in this world even if they do not have the power to subdue you. Sometimes it is their knowledge and imagination that will give you the advantage in a situation. Power and strength are only one piece to the puzzle that leads to true greatness. Compassion by far can take you much further." ShadowDancer gently pulled the threads back releasing Oondoheru from the binding. "You have been asleep for several millennia. Take the time and observation necessary to learn the world you are in."

"You are much more powerful than anyone I have met before." Luumeheru observed. "I would not venture to speculate a comparison. I expected the use of power to be more like ours or that of Felps here."

"Felps is a wizard or mage depending upon who you talk to. They do work similar to the way you do. They work though ritual and objects to manipulate the power they can access. Unlike you, they spend their lives working on refining the precision and control of that power to make it do what they want without the big splash or random fallout effect you have."

"We will have to work on that perhaps Felps, you can mentor me in some of these skills of focus." Luumeheru inquired.

"I would be glad to, but first we need to accommodate the needs of the Baratir. I am sure we did not bring them here to dump them in a strange world and let them wander aimlessly." Felps gestured to the subdued army and commander Breltak standing there with them.

"Breltak, you and your people are a remnant of a past time and represent the survival of your species and ways. I have proposed we create a continent and help you establish yourselves in a new start. Will your people follow you and accept things if you agree?" Lyamy took the lead in asking.

"I am their military commander, and they have no civilian lives currently to return. They will follow me at least until we can establish a village and set things in order according to our traditional ways. Then they will follow a council of elders who will honor any agreements that precede their assumption of power until such time they decide they need renegotiation."

*   *   *   *

*

Delmar looked at Lyamy. "So, you are saying that the event we prepared for has passed. It effected the shrine camp, but things are settled down and we no longer need to respond?"

"Exactly. Now I must depart, but Cellina will remain as the priestess for Sein Estel." Lyamy said as she stood up to leave.

Peltricia stood with her. "We will honor what we have learned during this crisis."

"Do not patronize me Peltricia. I like ShadowDancer can see the intent of your inner thoughts. Your choices are your own to make without trying to deceive me when I am here. Do what you will. Cellina will speak if you need warning or guidance."

"I serve to honor ShadowDancer." Cellina stated in a soft voice.

Lyamy looked at her. "Stay in peace." She faded and was gone. The secret room where she could view events through windows to places around the world vanished from Sein Estel with her. Lyamy pulled herself back together from almost all the locations. She remained in three locations on Ethar and one in her private universe. After what happened during her first meeting with Corvuset she had decided she would never be in just one place again.

Lyamy, ShadowDancer and Darvarias who had come to help them flew high above the ground. There was some debate as to where would be the best place to raise a continent to house the Baratir. In the end they decided to place it north of the savage continent where they would be isolated from the most active trade routes. A place where they could be isolated and establish their own culture before having to adjust to dealing with the races of the rest of the world.

To the north on the northern continent resided the oldest of the current civilizations on Ethar. They practiced an isolation from the rest of the world and would not impose on the Baratir. To the south while currently expanding the culture of the savage continent was working on its own identity and would be more interested in their connection to the civilized world through Kelleeshia then exploring relations with the new race until invited.

The three of them began the process of shifting land and water to raise the new continent from the ocean floor without causing abrupt destructive waves form any sudden change. They had the ability to move quickly swapping water for underwater rock and mass they moved to create land. Part of their goal was to create more land without changing the mass or stability of the world of Ethar. The trade-off was to make parts of the oceans deeper.

*   *   *   *

*

ShadowDancer and Lyamy bid farewell to Samuel and Terriala before heading with HonorLord, Darvarias, the wizard lords and the Baratir army back to the valley where they first arrived. The army was not in a battle fever, so they moved significantly slower than when they arrived. As they traveled though they were getting visibly more relaxed and casual conversation started between the drafted soldiers. From the conversations she overheard, the Baratir were anxious to get back to building from the land and away from killing and destruction.

Lyamy slipped down into the crowd moving from group to group asking questions about their lifestyle, the land they came from and the houses they lived in. She asked about the land they lived in. As she conversed with the Baratir she touched their minds and got a feel for the lives they lived. The images she got from their memories were houses framed with natural wood and stretched with animal hides. The land around them was red rock and dirt with random water springs that each created a small oasis of life. Down from the rock shelves they lived on were a variety of other landscapes from wetlands to forests. There were also caverns in the rock where they also built homes and house tents where they set up their businesses.

The information she was gathering would help them shape the land to a habitat that was familiar enough they might find comfort. While she was gathering information on the Baratir ShadowDancer and HonorLord were drawing information from Luumeheru and Oondoheru.

"So, what you are saying is you are all capable of learning each other's abilities with varied degrees of success. You choose to work that which comes most naturally to you." HonorLord was evaluating their methods. "Then you have all this power with manipulating stone and you just apply that to everything you do, but you never take the time to refine the skill?"

"Actually, we do take time to study and learn more about what we can do with our skills. Long ago when I first grew, I started by being able to throw big stones out of nowhere. From that I learned to do other things like clouds of stone, from that rain of stone sending the cloud over an enemy. As I became more powerful the bigger the effects of what I did." Oondoheru seemed proud of what he could do.

"That has value, but than you would not be able to select a single target and create a small stone cloud, say to fill a volcanic exhaust hole that threatened your people because if you did you would also hit them with the storm?" HonorLord capped the thought.

"Among your people though you had those who could also use magic at a much weaker scale and their skill were helpful to the village life of your tribes. Those who had the same magic as you were able to make stone bowls and utensils and they worked on refining and detailing those skills, but you never considered that with the power you wielded?" ShadowDancer was a bit befuddled at the lack of maturing in the thought processes of these titans of magic. To her they acted like young children playing their games of war with no consideration for anything outside the game. They also seemed to think the bigger the bang the more fun they were having.

"I have done more thinking since I woke up than I can remember doing before. What you say makes sense. All of the wizard lords that are waking up were the same way and probably still are. Luumeheru opened my eyes some which is why I tried to delay our return as long as I could.

250

You have opened my eyes to the ignorance we still have."

"We can feel where others like us are." ShadowDancer stated. "Can you tell where other wizard lords are?"

"Only if they are close enough." Luumeheru answered. "When we stayed back from the battlegrounds and did our part form a distance, we could not tell where others were who did the same. Forgive me for saying this, but at the time it made the battle more fun, not knowing who lead the current enemy forces."

"So currently you really don't know who if anyone has awakened in other parts of the world. The only way we will know is if they exercise their power or if one of you walks close enough to alert them you are there."

The conversation waxed long with little to gain advantage of trying to find the other wizard lords. Some knowledge was gained as far as what to expect in battle. The focus of conversation changed as they approached ground zero of the time collision. They arrived without incident at the plateau that filled what was previously a vast rich valley. The ground was uneven red stone with pockets of dirt and plants not native to the forest around them.

Lyamy reached out with her mind. "I can feel and separate the collision mass from the original. They have not yet merged beyond separation, although there will be some residual remnants that cross between the two."

"You have grown a lot." Darvarias commented, "I dare say you have studied what you can do with diligence."

"You capture it and I will help move the temporal displacement to the new continent." ShadowDancer nodded her approval.

HonorLord perceived their intent. "This is an event of Ethar a part of the order of events in the course of time. Is it safe to make so great a change?"

ShadowDancer smiled. "We are not going back and changing what has already happened, we are simply moving the consequences around a little. We are also part of the course of events and time on Ethar. The temporal realm will show us the fixed points that are not safe to disrupt."

"Even occasionally we may adjust those if we are willing to pay the price." Lyamy added, then shivered remembering the pain of being disassembled into the material needed to repair the breach in the temporal realm. It was a strange feeling even now, because while at the time she thought she was sacrificing the life of the one split of herself she did not die as she had first expected. She was still alive in the temporal mass holding the breach together. If she ever pulled that part of herself back it would disrupt millions of time threads. In a way while it saddled her with the continual burden of pulling and binding the temporal fabric, it also gave her an assurance of ongoing life. If somehow every copy of herself she was living outside the temporal focus were to die, she could pull herself back and re-spawn from her form that was locked in the time threads. If something tried to pull her life back out of the weaving of time, all of time would fight to keep her alive.

252

"We paid a price to change the course of events and spare these people from extermination." Luumeheru stated, "Only time will let us know if it was worth the price. Perhaps it was the only thing the immortals from our time ever did that was worth the price."

"Immortals?" HonorLord sounded offended. "Do you know what immortal means? Have any among your '*immortals*' ever died? As long as I can be made subject to death, I may live forever, but am not immortal. Immortality is a divine characteristic of a true God and while to some we may seem as such we are not and should not exalt ourselves as such."

"I did not mean to stir your anger." Luumeheru did not know how to further respond to the dissertation on immortality. He had never given much serious thought to the reference.

After a few moments of silence HonorLord realized how obtuse his outburst was. "Forgive me. You did nothing wrong. Immortal is a reference that is frequently used in reference to longevity beyond a recognizable natural mortality. I was never comfortable with being called immortal before I lost my wife. I may be oversensitive to the knowledge we are still subject to mortality."

"We have power and responsibility, we are not better than those we help, but we can make much more devastating mistakes." ShadowDancer looked at the powerful beings from the past. "If we do not stay humble, we will not be controlling the power we have, it will be controlling us."

"You have something we never had, wisdom." Oondoheru laughed. "In the short time I have been with you, I have had to think more than I did possibly in the entire time before. All we did was play a game pitting races against each other in wars that had no meaning. You give purpose to the lives of the races who serve you."

Lyamy shook her head. "The words you use may not seem like much, but they do not serve us, we help them. There are some who choose to serve maybe, but not because we make them and even they have to make that choice every time they do anything who or what they serve. Do not get me wrong there have been specific occasions where I have made someone do my will. We all learn to do better."

"See, wisdom. You think. You consider words. You see details. You use power with precision, we accept collateral damages." Oondoheru obviously approved of the change in thinking.

Luumeheru had a more somber expression. "It was my fault the destruction of our world. I learned to manipulate time. My armies could walk through solid walls by shifting time to when the wall was not there as they walked through. I learned to move my people forward and back through time and then also my enemies. I learned that the world moves because if you do not move with it with respect to the time you shift, seconds through time can move you miles from where you started. If you shift far enough through time without anchoring to a physical location, you shift things out into the dark of the stars above."

"So how are you responsible?" Lyamy asked when he took a breath.

Luumeheru continued leaving it indiscernible as to whether

Lyamy's question impacted what he said. "I learned to apply the magic of time in ways that should never be used. One day a young wizard lord came to me and asked to be my apprentice. At the time I did not know he served a counsel of my enemies. The day I taught him how to access the powers of time, I did not know they were using him to scry on the lesson. The moment he actuated the power of time he was summoned away. I taught the world of wizard lords how to access the magic of time. This had a cascading effect to the point of self-destruction. So, my fault for teaching how to use the power that destroyed us."

They had reached the middle of the plateau and ShadowDancer stopped and turned to Luumeheru. "You have a hard lesson there if you learned, but you did not cause the destruction. At best you chose the method. The self-centered abuse of power without regard for anyone else by the majority of the wizard lords assured destruction. You only provided the detail of how, the particular option that was used. That is not even your fault as much as it was stolen from you."

ShadowDancer nodded to Lyamy and a bubble formed around the entirety of the area effected by the time collision. The bubble rose up and once high enough to clear the mountain tops began a lateral movement to the west. Both Luumeheru and Oondoheru looked at them with amazement. They worked with clarity and precision. The movement was controlled and articulately adjusted as needed. They passed out over the walled city of Talmorg and over open sea.

Everyone remained silent during they moved. The Baratir all

dropped to their hands and knees. Lyamy was not sure if they were doing it in honor and respect or if they were just holding on uncertain of their destiny. ShadowDancer laughed in her mind, their thoughts linked to coordinate their effort. "You have not received worship before. Do not let it take away your humility." ShadowDancer spoke openly. "It can be difficult to not exalt yourself above people who are exalting you. I hope it might be easier for you, you know where you came from and even still are. You can never return to being the Lyamy that died to save her clan. To stay Lyamy of your den at the sanctuary, you must keep her separate from Lyamy the Ancient. These people worship us, you because of the power they do not see or understand."

"How did you know I could handle this much power and responsibility?"

"You have always been hard when you needed to and got things done that had to be done, but you have always been guided by compassion. Your compassion will keep you honest with yourself."

Luumeheru interjected. "I thought compassion was my weakness. It was how I discovered time magic, sparing my people from death. Other wizard lords had no problem sending thousands to their death which gave them a strength to wage war without regret or hesitation."

"Why do you think I mastered the power over stone?" Oondoheru shook his head. "Stone can shield and protect. To spare my people I sank villages into the stone and brought them back when the enemy was clear. There is a reason we were outcast my friend."
256

"And you still did not see us 'little people' when we first met?" ShadowDancer mocked. "And you are more enlightened than the rest of the wizard lords. I dare say we will have our hands full. We can not assume they are all evil, but they are at least as blind as the Ancients were before the few saw more then game pieces in the races here."

"You demonstrated power. That I can not fathom. You are saying you do not see the others as inferior." Oondoheru seemed still puzzled. "I have compassion for them and see they have minds to think and feel pain. They still have no power and even as they are a higher life form than the animals in the forest, we are a higher life form than they are."

Lyamy was taking some offense to the analogy. "So, are you saying whoever has more power is a higher life form? Then you concede ShadowDancer to be a higher life form then you? Or perhaps you are saying that the quantitative ability to understand being measurably greater makes a higher life form and your inability to understand how we see others would then qualify you as a lower life form still?"

"Be careful little one. I was not defeated by any of you. I concede that some of you if not your entire group may be on a par with me as far as power and if I do not agree with you that does not mean I do not understand." Oondoheru was grumbling with irritation at her verbal assault. "Do you challenge me and think you may overcome me with as much ease as anyone of us can overcome a member of the lesser races?"

"You do not wish to learn the outcome of such a challenge. Until you can show the humility of understanding, I cast my vote against teaching you to use the power you have with more skill." Lyamy drew back her anger, this was not the time or place. There was a lot of work to be done. "When the time comes perhaps, I will be the one to teach you."

Oondoheru was taken back by her confidence. She had seen some of his power and was not intimidated in the least. She actually had enough confidence to turn her back on him and calm her own anger. ShadowDancer had stopped him with no sign of outward effort, perhaps he was not a real threat to this Lyamy either. He put his anger in check. "We will see when the time is right. It will take time for me to know what has changed in the world and what if anything is the same." He could not sense the presence of their power as could with other of the wizard lords, so neither could he measure their strength.

They approached the new continent. There was a hollow in the middle of the continent as they passed from the coast over wetlands and forest and reached the massive stone plateau in the middle. Forward movement slowed until they were at a stop. Then they started moving downwards at a fairly good clip slowing down as they approached full closure of the distance. Considering the mass they were moving it was a gentle thump as they dropped into place, although a few of the soldiers lost their balance enough to scuffle back onto all fours.

ShadowDancer raised her hand open palmed in a gesture telling the masses to rise and they obeyed. The transition between the displaced mass of ground and stone to the continent around it was not visible to the eye. Darvarias, ShadowDancer and Lyamy pulled back their doubles from

258

the island before anyone took notice. Lyamy knew from looking in their minds before what materials they needed to rebuild in the same fashion as the village they previously lived in. She summoned enough materials for them to build their shelters sufficient for everyone present. It appeared stacked just outside the masses in an orderly fashion on the ground.

Enhancing her voice so all could here without having to use volume Lyamy spoke. "We will provide for your needs until you are established sufficiently to provide for yourselves. This continent was made for you. You will have time to establish yourselves before you have to contend with the other races of the world."

ShadowDancer added, "We will also be sending you others displaced from your time. They are no longer enemies, so you will accept them as members or help them build a community as allies." The Baratir would treat anyone as a friend unless they proved otherwise, and the numbers of the other fugitives were not sufficient for them to do anything more than accept that hospitality. The Baratir had also not been in the wars long enough to have any grudge enemies.

"Commander Breltak lead your people to their new life well. We have things to attend to elsewhere. One of us will hear when you call." Lyamy gave a slight bow of her head giving the commander respect.

He returned the bow significantly more elaborate and acknowledged them all. "I shall help them establish a new council and build shelters. We are a free people no longer in service to a wizard lord."

"Now we must find those that are awakening and protect the

world." Luumeheru stated.

"We have much more than that to do." HonorLord nodded. "We still have to finish cleaning up the spray of consequences from the time displacement. I am going back to the home continent of ShadowKeep starting from there."

"I am going to start a council." ShadowDancer stated. "In three days, we will meet. I will provide the place, but I wish you and your son to be there. I will be gathering those with power who still have an active interest in the events of Ethar. You two will also be invited." She gestured to Luumeheru and Oondoheru.

"We will be honored." Luumeheru replied

Eric her father appeared at her side. "We will be there. It is the right time, daughter."

"Father, you could have formed a council to keep order among those with power a long time ago." ShadowDancer said a little sharper than she intended.

"You are of this world, I am not. It is better this way. I could have claimed such authority and enforced it, but I would have been an outsider. It is your world, and you will have the acceptance and approval to accomplish agreement."

He was right. She already had support from corners that he would have had to stand against. Those who were not already a party to events would not have been pleased to yield to someone they did not feel was from Ethar. "Forgive my sharpness, father."

260

"You do not need my forgiveness. There are dozens of mistakes I have made to earn at the very least an occasional quip from you."

*   *   *   *

*

King Tagmerian was eating his afternoon crackers and sipping tea while reading and signing or rejecting paperwork. The guard stepped in and announced Lyamy and company. The entourage entered as directed.

"It is good to see you again Lyamy. Although I must say there was a time when I would not believe those words would ever come out of my mouth."

Lyamy bowed halfway and indicated for the rest of those with her to bow. "It is good to see the kingdom doing so well and to find you in good health." Pointing to each and having them step forward in turn she introduced each member of the two families. As she did so King Tagmerian advised each of the adults what jobs he was offering them in the Palace.

When the introductions were complete, he called Mathew forward. "Mathew, I have been given wise council that I need to choose and train an heir since I am beyond having children of my own and the kingdom will need someone wise and in touch with the people to rule when I am gone. Lyamy has advised me that you would be a good selection. If you accept this position you will spend a lot of time in training. You will continue to live with your family here in the palace, but the majority of your time would be spent learning from books and learning the art of war and combat. Does that sound like a choice you are ready to make?”

“If Lyamy said I should, she has saved my family and is really smart, I would listen to her advice and accept.” Mathew looked a little nervous and excited at the same time. “I hope that I can prove to do a good job.”

King Tagmerian followed Lyamy’s recommendations and provided positions and jobs for the two families in the palace. He was not without opposition and conflict in his kingdom, but the kingdom would last and conditions for the people were getting better.

*   *   *   *

*

The Wizard Lords from the past were gathered. Once ShadowDancer, Lyamy, ant the others close to ShadowDancer examined the power of the Wizard lords they knew, they figured out how to locate the others. Eric shared access to the planet where he had been moving those that would have died in space and the rest to the fallout that was spread off world. All of the Wizard Lords were moved there and learned they were not as powerful as they had thought themselves to be. They were educated on the history of the Ancients as far as respecting races, and those who chose to follow the rules on Ethar were given the option of becoming part of the world. Others were allowed to start fresh on the world Eric created knowing they would be subject to his authority.

Having settled in her traveling companions to their new lives Lyamy sought out Corvuset and Cellina. They were to be a part of

ShadowDancer's council. The council was something that ShadowDancer had been working on in concept for a while. Any ancient or being of a higher power level than normal mortals who wished to have any participation in the events of Ethar would be required to be a member of her council. This would not be just those with good intent.

She determined that if people were to be free, they had to have opportunity to make choices including to serve good or evil and possibly anything in between. The participation of non-mortals or immortals in the events of the world would be primarily through influence, not direct action. Exceptions would be at ShadowDancer's discretion. In some cases, she may delegate that discretion.

There were mortals from every continent that she picked to be on her council. The world did not know what was being orchestrated, but the freedom that was being walked in would be protected. The choices the people made would have effect on the world and the people around them, but choices and direction would be determined by the peoples of the world, not mandated by their Ancients or gods.

There would be transitioning and the distinction between mortal powers and immortal powers was in places not a clear line. ShadowDancer would be recognized as final authority in matters governing the influences of the races. She had to learn to keep balance and allow things she disapproved of in order to protect the freedom of choice. How can a goddess of such power allow such bad things to happen? If she is truly good, how could she not allow her peoples the freedom to choose?

She was a self-appointed goddess of Ethar with the power to bring the other powers under her authority. She also had the support of the elders of the ancients that came before her and the backing of the strength of her father who as far as she understood was more powerful than any of the others. She had the support of all of the ancients of the new order when it came to matters of this world. ShadowDancer also cared about the people, this was her world.

The New Council:

Leader: Ancient and Goddess of Ethar – ShadowDancer

Lyamy – right hand of ShadowDancer, Avatar, Ancient, directly involved living with the people of Ethar, allowed to act with the authority of ShadowDancer.

Family

Eric Marland – council and adviser, not subject to any

Bonny Marland – Ancient of Healing, council and adviser, not subject to any

Franklin and Roxanne Marland – Sister and brother to ShadowDancer, not of Ethar, allowed to act under the tutelage of ShadowDancer.

Advisory members of the council

Drakalon – Old One Council of dragons

Keltoe – Old One council of dragons(Leader of the Old Ones)

Gaharias – Elder of the ancients head of the council of ancients

Darvel – Elder of the ancients head of the dark council

HonorLord/Hans Spardic – Ancient of War, voluntarily subject to

ShadowDancer in matters of Ethar

Jaharadan – ancient of necromancy

Luumeheru – Wizard Lord

Oondoheru – Wizard Lord

Corvuset – Rogue Ancient

Darvarias – New Ancient

Cadabriana creature of death – Changeling from the time of legends

Some of the other ancients joined many moved on no longer interested in

the affairs of Ethar.

Others of the old ones (lord dragons) agreed to consult with

ShadowDancer before taking any action, some simply moved on or chose

to slumber for a few millennium

9 781966 954521